FOOTSTEPS IN THE DARK.
MAYBE YOU LOOK, MAYBE YOU DON'T. . . .

"Finally, despite everything you've been telling yourself, you can't help it—you look. You don't want to, but you look."

She waited, then said at last, "And?"

"There's no one back there, of course. The street is still empty. Still dark. Nothing back there at all."

Her left hand moved unconsciously to close her coat at the neck.

"But there *were* footsteps," she said, not quite a question.

"Oh, yes. There were. There are always footsteps."

She made to speak, then shook her head and left.

He waited until he heard her car back out of the driveway. Then he put the flyer he'd been holding in his lap and opened it. *All Are Welcome* was printed across the bottom, flanked by a pair of well-drawn wings.

Leona Elmdorf had harshly circled one of the wings several times with a dark pen, and had drawn an arrow to the margin. When he turned the paper over, there was another note:

These aren't angels' wings, Mr. Proctor. Don't be fooled. You only hear these *wings at night.*

BLACK OAK 2

THE HUSH OF DARK WINGS

by

Charles Grant

A ROC BOOK

ROC
Published by the Penguin Group
Penguin Putnam Inc., 375 Hudson Street,
New York, New York 10014, U.S.A.
Penguin Books Ltd, 27 Wrights Lane,
London W8 5TZ, England
Penguin Books Australia Ltd, Ringwood,
Victoria, Australia
Penguin Books Canada Ltd, 10 Alcorn Avenue,
Toronto, Ontario, Canada M4V 3B2
Penguin Books (N.Z.) Ltd, 182–190 Wairau Road,
Auckland 10, New Zealand

Penguin Books Ltd, Registered Offices:
Harmondsworth, Middlesex, England

First published by Roc, an imprint of Dutton NAL,
a member of Penguin Putnam Inc.

First Printing, January, 1999
10 9 8 7 6 5 4 3 2 1

 REGISTERED TRADEMARK—MARCA REGISTRADA

Printed in the United States of America

For Laura Anne, the patient saint.

Previously, in *Black Oak*

On a mist-shrouded highway in eastern Kentucky, Ethan Proctor asks his companion:

"Do you believe in ghosts?"

On a private jet, somewhere over Virginia: Taylor Blaine speaks to Ethan Proctor about the reason for their meeting:

"We were in Connecticut, Mr. Proctor. The family home. It was late June. Celeste had just turned eighteen. Nineteen eighty-four, it was. She was to attend Wellesley that fall, and was going to travel a little with two of her friends before locking herself away behind ivy-covered walls. We had been joking about George Orwell and such, because of the year. She was afraid Big Brother would take over sooner or later. I was of the opinion he already had.

"I stood on the front porch and watched the three of them drive away. They were laughing, Mr. Proctor, waving out the windows and laughing.

"She called her mother every other night for the

next two weeks. Every other night, Mr. Proctor, but I never saw her again.

"Two years later, my Iris passed away. A massive stroke in the middle of the night. I am convinced it was the pressure of not knowing.

"Whatever the reason, they're both gone now.

"One, I have lost forever.

"I want the other one back."

"Here is the deal," Blaine said. "It's very simple, don't look so apprehensive. You will allow me to hire Black Oak—which means you, sir; you—to find out what happened to my daughter. I will pay all your expenses, I will give you access to every one of my contacts as they become necessary, I will give you the run of my house, my offices wherever they may be, and my staff. I will give you free reign to do whatever you want, whatever it takes.

"In addition, I will pay you enough above and beyond so that you will never have to work on anything else in your life."

Blaine held out his hand.

Proctor didn't take it.

"If I accept," Proctor told him, "I will run my business as usual. I have clients, sir, who depend on me and my people. And frankly, this case is so old . . . the odds against the results you're looking for are great."

"Great," Blaine echoed mockingly. "What you mean is, a hell of a hell of a hell of a hell of a long shot. Snowball in hell. Slim to none, and slim is out of the question.''

"Yes, sir, that is exactly what I mean.''

Blaine's hand didn't retreat.

"And you have to work,'' he said thoughtfully. "Other cases, that is. My daughter's . . . my daughter will be just one case among many.''

Proctor nodded. "Yes, I do have to work. I'd go nuts if I didn't. Even with all those reports and contacts and whatever of yours, there's going to be a lot of downtime. Time when I'll be just twiddling my thumbs, as it were. I can't live like that. Your own story tells me you can't either. Which tells me you don't like it, but you do understand.''

Blaine returned his gaze steadily.

For the first time, Proctor looked at the hand, then looked up. "But your daughter will *not* be just one case among many. None of my cases are, Mr. Blaine. None.''

The plane touched the runway with a faint lurch and squeal, both men were eased forward when the engines reversed and the brakes were applied, and Proctor, without thinking, took the old man's hand.

Blaine's smile broadened; his grip was snug without testing.

"You won't regret this, Ethan,'' he said.

"It's Proctor,'' Proctor said. "Nobody calls me Ethan. And yeah, sure I'm going to regret this. You and I, we're going to fight like cats and dogs.''

do you believe in ghosts?

Episode 2

THE HUSH OF
DARK WINGS

ONE

There were stars, and a waning moon, and a touch in the air of thin brittle ice.

There was darkness laced with silver.

And the hush of a light cold wind that passed through the high buffalo grass. Whispers in the night. The souls of the dead, locals liked to say, the Indians and settlers who had lived and traveled on the Great Plains, plotting ways to return. No ghostly moans, no banshee screams, no clank and clatter of chains dragged behind.

Only the whispering, constant and soft.

And the irregular harsh panting of someone who has run a long way, who can barely move another step, who needs to sit a while and rest and doesn't dare.

Kira wished desperately she could stay off the road. She could hide in the tall grass, or find a depression to crouch in, or maybe there'd be a miracle and she'd find a cave somewhere along the weed-choked banks of one of the long-dead creeks, where she could wait until the sun rose and everything would be all right.

But there were no miracles, not anymore, and the stars and the moon didn't give a damn.

Just the night long past midnight, and the dry cold wind that, slow as it was, still made her feel as if she weren't wearing any clothes.

Besides, she thought bitterly, running across the plains in the middle of the night was a blatant invitation to certain disaster—a turned ankle, a broken leg, or something worse: getting lost.

The paved two-lane road allowed her to move swiftly, at least in the beginning, and it led straight toward home, waiting for her up there, somewhere in the faint glow that marked what was left of Hart Junction. Maybe Kenny would still be there. Maybe he hadn't given up on her. Maybe he was waiting in the living room, a lamp on in the window, watching TV and once in a while glancing at the door in case she should come home.

She had to believe that.

If she didn't, if she couldn't, there was no sense going on, she might as well sit down right here and let it happen.

A sudden stitch of pain in her right side made her gasp aloud, and she slowed to a stumbling walk, finally stopped and bent over as she massaged the place where she hurt. A few seconds wouldn't kill her; a few seconds, that's all, until the pain went away.

She had long since gotten used to the rest of it— the vicious scrapes on her knees when she'd fallen and skidded at the beginning of her flight, tearing open jeans and flesh; the dozens of scratches and a handful of cuts on the backs of her hands and across her cheeks when she'd tried, really tried, to use the buffalo grass for cover and fallen too many times before realizing the futility and had taken to the road.

If she bled, she couldn't tell. The cold had numbed her skin, made the aches go away. For a while, anyway. For a while.

In her left hand was a flashlight. She used it sparingly, flick on and flick off, just to be sure she wasn't heading for the shallow ditches that bordered the road. Use it more than that and they would find her without half trying. A single light in all this emptiness could be seen for too many miles.

After a few seconds the pain subsided, she grunted, and moved on. Slower now, screaming silently at her legs not to give up, there were only two miles or so left, more than halfway home. And once there, she swore, she would never leave the house again, not until she had convinced Kenny that their future lay somewhere, anywhere else, but definitely not in Hart Junction.

It would be hard. He could be so damn stubborn sometimes. Handsome, smart, but with the genes of a damn mule. Once she told him what she had seen, however, she doubted he'd argue. He would do what she wanted.

He had to.

Please, God, he had to.

A flick of the light, the blacktop washed a temporary grey, and she picked up the pace again, staggering from one side of the road to the other but not once taking her gaze off the glow up ahead.

Sweat drenched her hair, soaked her back. Cramps stirred in her thighs. She wasn't sure, but she thought she felt blood slipping down her shins. Her jacket, an old leather thing she had worn when she'd left home, gained a pound with every step, but she didn't dare take it off.

The wind gusted, nearly toppling her.

The whispers rose and fell.

She gulped a breath, and dropped the flashlight when her fingers stopped working.

"Shit," she muttered wearily as she turned, listening to the plastic casing rattle across the blacktop. She was tempted to leave it, but she had to have it. Slip into one of the ditches and she was a goner. "Shit," and she dropped to her knees, inhaling sharply at the stinging, the burning, forcing herself to ignore it as she passed her hands over the gritty surface until she found the light, giggled, and tried to stand again.

She couldn't.

Her knees wouldn't lock, her arms had lost their strength, and she fell back onto her rump.

Okay, she thought, not giving panic a chance; okay, this is a sign, right? Body says I have to rest or it ain't moving again. No sweat.

She giggled, and wiped the sweat from her face with a forearm.

No sweat, I can handle it.

The wind stopped.

The whispering stopped.

Her wheezing sounded like the pitiful roar of an aged lion.

Okay, it's okay, count to ten and get up off your butt, Kira Marie Stark, this ain't a vacation, you know. It ain't fun and games. And the first thing you're going to do when you get home is beat the hell out of your pigheaded husband for not stopping you, the jerk.

Or coming after you, the bastard.

She giggled.

Then you are going to take the longest bath you've ever had in your life, in the history of the world, eat everything in the refrigerator that isn't covered with some kind of fungus because Kenny never did have the sense to throw things out when they needed throwing out, and then you are going to pack, drag him to the car, and drive as far away as you can, the hell with trying to convince him there's something wrong. If he hasn't figured that out by now, he deserves to stay behind.

She giggled.

She put a trembling hand over her eyes, took as deep a breath as her lungs would allow, and replaced another giggle with an explosive sob of exhaustion, and the fear that she was cracking up. So tired of running, so tired of listening to *them* talking to her, so tired of listening to what was left of her mind tell her she was—

Her hand snapped away, and she scrambled awkwardly to her feet, swaying.

Out there in the dark.

Something was out there.

She was positive she had heard it, but she couldn't hear it now, no matter how hard she strained to listen over the frantic thumping of her heart and the wheezing as she breathed through her open mouth.

It wasn't the wind; there was no wind.

She stepped backward, stepped again, squinting hard into the dark, holding the flashlight like a club. It couldn't be them, because she would have heard them. Either they'd be in that fancy car, the only vehicle they owned, or they'd be running just like her; either way, she would have heard.

"No time to stop," she whispered. Her arms at her sides were too heavy to move. "Go, Kira, damnit, move."

She couldn't.

Nothing worked.

Standing with her legs apart, blinking rapidly, gulping air, she cocked her head and listened, closed her eyes and listened harder. Smiled. Giggled. Wiped the back of her hand across her lips and swiveled around stiff-legged, fixed on the Junction's glow and let it pull her forward. One small step at a time, legs unbending, reminding her so much of Frankenstein that she grinned, growled, and tried to imagine what the bolt-neck monster would look like, running.

Dear Lord, I'm cracking up.

Kenny, help me, I'm cracking up, oh God, I'm not gonna make it.

She heard Kenny's voice, that smooth deep voice,

telling her to stop feeling so damn sorry for herself. She was a grown woman, damn near thirty, and since she'd gotten herself into this mess, she could damn well get herself out. All she had to do was stop thinking about the aches, the pains, the lead in her muscles, the burning in her lungs.

Don't think about it.

Just do it.

So she did, just to prove to that goddamn smug bastard that she didn't need him, didn't need anyone, to get her out of anything. Three-quarters dead on her feet, she was still better than half the men who still lived in the Junction, hiding behind their doors each time the sun went down, holding meetings that accomplished nothing, writing letters that were never answered, all the while carrying on as if there was nothing wrong. Going to work, coming home, everything's okay, Kira, it's all in your mind, your pretty little head.

Like the sound she heard again, somewhere out there. This time she didn't stop.

It wasn't them.

It couldn't be them.

It was the whispers, all those dead Indians and pioneers, except . . . except the wind wasn't blowing.

Scowling, she glanced over her shoulder, thinking she could tear apart the dark with just a look and expose whoever was back there. Whatever was back there. It didn't occur to her to use the flashlight for another hundred yards, and when she did, she wished she hadn't.

The beam wasn't very strong, the night was much stronger, but it was enough to show her the long empty road. She swung the light right to left quickly, hoping to catch the glint of an eye or a ducking shadow.

Nothing there; there was nothing there.

Yet she heard it, a rustling, a whispering, so soft and so constant that she couldn't decide whether to be angry or afraid.

"Screw it," she muttered, and turned toward the Junction, nodded at how wonderfully close it seemed, and took a step toward it.

The rustling grew louder.

The flashlight aimed at the tall grass that didn't move, that seemed like a solid wall wherever the beam touched it. She stabbed the beam elsewhere, thrusting out her arm as if wielding a sword, turning in an increasingly frantic circle until she tripped herself and fell, landing on her left hip, gasping, sighing, sitting up with one hand braced on the blacktop while the other used the flashlight.

The rustling grew louder, nearer, and she opened her mouth and said, "Oh," when she realized it wasn't the dead whispering at all.

What she heard was the sound of wings.

Soft wings.

Beating slowly.

Run, Kenny told her; for God's sake, Kira, run!

She couldn't; she couldn't even stand. But she wasn't dead yet, and she turned the flashlight back into a club, and batted blindly at the air above her, behind her, using her heels to turn her around, and turn her once again. Sobbing and not caring, wishing the tears hadn't blurred her vision because she was sure the slow-fading beam kept slashing over something out there, just out of reach.

Large or small, she couldn't tell.

A glimpse, nothing more.

And when the flashlight finally died and left her in the dark, the sound of soft wings settled over her.

Without even time for a single frightened scream.

TWO

The sun was too bright, the temperature too high, and Ethan Proctor almost smiled when he found himself yearning for a little tried-and-true November gloom. Damp and grey, to keep you under the blankets for just a few minutes more.

The idea had been a good one at the time: Get out of the office for a while, take a walk down to Parker Street, pick up a couple of doughnuts from the Italians who owned the Swiss Bakery, and munch his way back home. By then, his head would be clear, he would be invigorated from the exercise of the nearly mile-long journey, and he would finally be able to make a decision about the letter.

But as he stood on the sidewalk, a bag with three lemon-filled doughnuts in one hand, he felt more akin to Mr. Scrooge than Mr. Claus. Although the business district was only a few blocks long, the colorful decorations in the store windows and on the lampposts, the recorded carols he could just hear down the block, the pedestrians who flowed past him cheerfully burdened with packages and smiles, all seemed false in the sunlight.

It was November, for crying out loud, Thanksgiving four days gone, and there should be low grey clouds, a damp chilly breeze, and the sense that anything, even winter, would be better than the gloom.

But not, however, this damn summer weather.

Scrooge, he thought, shook his head, and walked left, keeping close to the storefronts, away from the crowds, glaring at the traffic that clogged the street in both directions. At the corner, taken by Munshin's Books, he turned left again and paused. The outside of the bookstore's display window had been given over to posters and announcements, both hand-lettered and professionally done. Local bands at local clubs, school plays and concerts, town-sponsored events, block parties, a Christmas concert at the VFW, lost pets, lost wallets, lost toys, lost people.

He spotted a vivid yellow sheet in the center on the right-hand edge: an invitation to a meeting at someone's house, the speaker a man who claimed to have an indisputable and active pipeline to God. The leader of a group that called itself Angel Watch. All were welcome, young and old, the distressed and the lost, the wondering and the aimlessly wandering.

He scowled, automatically reached out to rip the paper away, and changed his mind. For one thing there was Munshin's rule—what goes up stays up unless he takes it down, no matter how stupid or offensive others might find it. Besides, it wouldn't make any difference anyway. Proctor had seen this same announcement elsewhere lately, on telephone poles, in the classified section of the local newspaper, in the hands of earnest youngsters standing on street corners passing them out.

It wouldn't make any difference.

And as he walked away, heading east toward his own neighborhood, he wondered if he ought to consider this a sign.

Dear Mr. Proctor,

Several years ago, you helped my cousin, Betty Savage, maybe you remember her, with a I guess you'd call it a sticky problem. She always told me, before she died of that cancer, that if I ever needed help too, I should contact you. It never occurred to me that I ever would. But I do.

Halfway home, working on his second doughnut, he considered taking off his denim jacket. It was too warm, and despite the fact that he was taking his time, he could feel sweat breaking on his back and under his arms.

The view was worse, too.

The only color belonged to the houses and the evergreens and a few patches of stubbornly green grass. The trees and most shrubs he could see were bare. Gardens were empty. Wreaths and bows on doors seemed made of plastic. Strings of lights around jambs and on bushes looked silly, pointless, in all this sun. The place needed darkness, for the lights to shine, or snow, to hide the barren limbs and browning lawns.

Damn, he thought; what the hell's the matter with you?

Part of his funk, he knew, was due to the recent death of an old friend, one of his investigators, who had been in Black Oak since the beginning. But that had been six weeks ago, and although the sting was still there, the memory of the man's passing and the way it had happened, it wasn't enough to make him feel like this.

You know, he told himself then; stop kidding yourself, you know what it is.

"Smart-ass," he muttered to his shadow with a lopsided grin.

When he reached the T-intersection at the end of the street, he crossed over and headed north. There was no sidewalk on this side, just a worn-to-bare-earth north-south path on a narrow irregular verge of low grass. It was this way for good reason—beyond the widely spaced houses on his right the land ended abruptly at the New Jersey Palisades, in spots several hundred feet straight down to the Hudson River. Those who lived in the large, old homes across the way saw little but high hedges or vine-entangled fences or trees which, in summer, blocked even the buildings.

Not much of a view, but the older residents didn't seem to mind, and the newer ones either got used to it or moved away.

As he finished his second doughnut, his right hand drifted to touch his hip pocket. Where the envelope was.

I haven't told anyone else because I'm frightened. Really frightened.

They all were, usually, those whose concerns and

appeals eventually made it through his various contacts to his combination home and office.

They all were.

The majority of Black Oak's investigations dealt with alleged fraud. Skimming. Diverting funds. Elaborate scams and schemes that weren't as foolproof as their inventors believed. The exposure of those who believed the world owed them a living and thought they had figured out how to make it pay through the nose.

He chose the cases, and supervised, but most of the actual work was done by the handful of people who worked with him.

He concentrated on other things.

A car passed him, heading south, a touch on its horn that brought his hand up in a wave even though he didn't know who the driver was.

A breeze-ruffled crow picked languidly at the remains of something in the road near the curb on the other side. He stamped his foot hard, but the bird only looked up, cocked its head, and fed on.

My kind of guy, he thought wryly. Like the objects of the cases he undertook himself—the scavengers. Palm readers and fortune-tellers, mystics and psychics; monsters in the attic and sometimes monsters in the soul; predators and prophets who claimed connections with the Beyond, Outer Space, Alternate Universes, Alternate Worlds, Benevolent Spirits and their Messages of Peace and Doom; ghosts and goblins and things that thump and bump around in the night.

Victims who had lost savings, lost relatives or friends, lost hope, lost will.

And he realized with a soundless sigh, watching the crow watching him, why his mood had turned.

We used to have a pretty nice town here, Mr. Proctor, it wasn't much to look at, we're way out in the back of nowhere, but a lot of good people called it home. But it isn't home anymore, not the way it used to be, not the way it was before they came around.

He never took cases like this one lightly. More often than not, they were only facades. Fancy or clumsy curtains that hid the true wizard in the Emerald City. The wizards, however, weren't all as fundamentally good-hearted or well-meaning as the man behind the levers and flashing lights in Oz. The Angel Watch announcement he had seen downtown, for example, might well be perfectly harmless, the leader absolutely sincere in his quest; it would depend on the group's tenets, the procedures . . . the cost of belief.

It was the charlatans who angered him, the pretenders and the purveyors of contemporary snake oil; and once they were exposed he didn't always turn them over to the police. Sometimes a slap on the wrist was only, in the end, a simple slap on the wrist.

But sometimes he had his own idea of what proper justice should be.

They took Vera, my sister, and I want her back. God knows she's not perfect, but she's all I have left, and I'm afraid for her.

Yet even the earnest pleas in letters like this didn't always move him. There were too many. Far too many, even with the filtering through people who knew him and his reputation. The only method he used to choose which to accept and which to deny was instinct, and even that wasn't perfect. Sometimes he was so wrong it was laughable. Infallibility was definitely not one of his traits.

But every so often . . .

I don't know how to put this any other way, but since you didn't laugh at Betty, I'm hoping you won't laugh at me either—I don't think these people are human, Mr. Proctor, and if they are, they have no human souls. Little by little they're taking my town apart. One by one. There aren't many of us left. Soon there won't be anyone left. I can't run, my car's broke down and I can't get around as well as I used to anyway.

Every so often . . .

So please let me know soon if you can do anything for me. For my town. For my sister.

He did, in fact, remember Elizabeth Savage, a years-ago case not long after he had started Black Oak. It had eventually taken him to . . . he frowned, scratched his cheek . . . somewhere in the upper Midwest, maybe, he wasn't really sure. A ghost, if he remembered correctly; a haunting that had turned out to be nothing more than a nephew who had more greed than sense. It hadn't been, at the last, all that difficult to unravel. He and the young man had had a short conversation the night it had ended. They had been outside, and the kid was truly contrite.

More greed than sense; his conscience would have done the job sooner or later.

No police, then.

But as Elizabeth had come out to the porch, wanting to know if everything was all right, Proctor had leaned close to the young man's ear, gripped his arm, and had whispered, "I'll be watching."

Nothing more.

He had never considered himself an imposing man. Not husky, no taller than average, dark sandy hair that stubbornly refused to stay out of his face. Maybe it was something in the tone, in the voice. Maybe, as he'd once heard his people say, it was the dark deep-set eyes. He didn't know. He didn't really care because thinking about it embarrassed him.

Whatever it was, however, as with Elizabeth's nephew, it was enough.

He took the envelope out, studied it, tapped it against his palm, and returned it to his hip pocket.

Okay, Leona, he thought to the writer.

He looked over his shoulder.

The crow was still there, still eating, and still watching.

Okay, Leona, yes, I'll do it.

Because every so often, the ghosts turn out not to be nephews at all.

THREE

Bill Albright fit the last suitcase into the trunk, slammed the lid extra hard just to be sure the latch caught, and looked over at the house. Anything there? Anything left behind? Should he take one last look around just in case he missed something important?

Too bad and too late and no way in hell; the car would barely hold him as it was, packed cheek to jowl with everything he could squeeze in.

All that mattered was that he got out of here.

He looked up and down the street, squinting into the setting sun. Nothing; there was nothing. Most of the houses were empty, and the block felt like it. Deserted and lifeless. All that was missing was a lone tumbleweed bouncing along the blacktop to complete the ghost-town image.

He shook his head once, pulled his keys from his hip pocket, and shook them hard, just for the noise. That's what he missed most around here—the constant noise. Dogs, cats, kids playing, people calling to each other, a lawn mower, a power saw, someone's radio playing too loud. Not just here, either, but from other streets too.

Sound carried in the Junction on the slow constant breeze, but there was nothing on the breeze now but dust and silence.

He almost felt bad, but not bad enough that he was going to stick around. The hell with it. The hell with them.

A final look at the house he had built himself, and he walked to the driver's door, opened it, and heard the footsteps behind him.

Damn, he thought.

With a smile he didn't feel, he turned to watch Leb Coster walk toward him, hands in his jeans, windbreaker open, scuffed boots with polished metal tips once in a while kicking at a pebble. Taking his time.

"Leaving?" Leb called.

No, Bill thought; I've decided to live out of my car, you stupid shit.

"Yep. Just going."

The man kicked at another pebble, sniffed, passed a finger under his nose. "You're sure, are you?"

"What do you think?"

Coster reached the car and leaned against the fender, peering through the windows at the stuff packed inside. Then he nodded toward the house. "Just gonna leave it, huh?"

Bill nodded impatiently.

"Not good business, Bill. Place'll fall apart."

"Like I care."

"A house needs somebody, you know? It ain't right, a house standing without somebody inside."

"Then you move in," he said, deliberately heavy on the sarcasm.

Coster smiled briefly. "Sorry. Got my own place, thanks." He pushed away from the car, checked the cloudless sky. "Got a proposition for you."

"Not interested."

"You in a hurry?"

Bill snorted. "You could say that."

"Got ten minutes for an old friend?"

He and Coster had never been friends; they just happened to live in the same two-bit town that had been dying on its feet for nearly twenty years. Still, he had heard rumors and stories, and he wondered.

"For what?"

"Ike wants to see you before you go."

Bill wasn't sure about that. Less than an hour before sunset, and he wanted to be on the road as soon as he could. He should have been out of here two hours ago, but the house had surprised him. It held more than he'd thought, and it had taken a while to fight through all the memories packed in all the corners. They hadn't changed his mind; they'd just surprised him, that's all.

He looked at his watch.

"Ten minutes," Coster said. "Swear to you, ten minutes."

Bill shrugged, and Coster walked away. "He's at the house."

Ten minutes.

He looked at the sun at the end of the street, slowly burning orange as dust rose from the plains.

Ten minutes.

A *what the hell* shrug, and he slammed the door, pocketed the keys. He didn't bother to lock it. There wasn't anything in there worth stealing, and there wasn't hardly anyone around to steal it anyway.

He followed Coster to a wide gap that formed a corner with the street. There were no regular north-to-south streets in the Junction, only alleys every four or five houses just wide enough for a single car. Some were rutted, all were worn, none were paved. Just hard-packed dirt and some stubborn grass and weeds. Because of the fences, the trees, the houses, the alleys were always in shade and shadow, more so now that the sun was on its way down.

Coster said nothing, didn't look back.

Bill wondered why the man stayed. It wasn't as if he was independently wealthy, and Bill didn't think he had much truck with the Morning Star freaks. Running a feed-and-grain store when there weren't any farms or ranches left, and only a few head of cattle and a couple of scrawny horses, wasn't the way to build an empire. Not around here. Not anymore.

So why did he stay?

At the end of the passage, they turned right and made their way to the second house along the way, two stories and wood, well kept, neat, even a lawn that this close to December held most of its green.

They went inside without knocking.

A half dozen men in the living room, all greeting

him with nods and smiles, a few expressions of regret that he was leaving but good luck in the future.

He followed Leb down a short hall into the kitchen.

Ike Wayman stood behind a butcher-block table, still in his expensive, probably tailored, three-piece suit. One of Bill's old girlfriends once remarked that the banker looked like a bowling pin, and the image had stuck no matter how hard he tried to shake it.

"Leaving, I see," Wayman said, held out his hand, and Bill shook it. "Sorry to hear it."

"The way it goes," Bill said, not really caring.

"Well." Wayman touched a point on his brow where his hairline dived to a sharp widow's peak. Rubbed it softly. "Do you have prospects, Bill? Where you're going, that is. You got things lined up okay?"

Albright was a carpenter and master cabinetmaker; he had never doubted he'd be able to find work wherever he landed.

"I'd like to help."

Bill looked at him askance.

Wayman laughed, a soft braying sound. "Truly, Bill." He opened the folder. "There's no sense letting good property go to waste is what I always say. After you leave, sooner or later someone might move in on his own, take over, so to speak. Maybe, someday, you'll want to return. To your roots, as they say." He slid the first page aside. "Then what we have is a classic hassle. Squatter versus rightful owner." He made a face. "Very nasty. Lawyers, and judges, and good money down the drain. Points of law. All that nonsense.''

The window behind the banker darkened.

"What's your point, Ike?" Bill asked.

"The point is, we'll buy your house," Wayman answered flatly. "The town, that is. Preserve it for posterity.''

Bill didn't get it. What the hell would the town, especially now, want with his house? On the other hand, this meant that the rumors and stories were true—Hart Junction was buying up the property people left behind.

Wayman reached into his jacket and pulled out an envelope. "This," he said, reaching across the table, "is a bank check. Good as cash. Can't be stopped, can't be taken back.''

Bill took it, looked at Leb, who was busy cleaning his nails with a toothpick, and opened it.

He blinked.

He blinked again.

Wayman laughed. "I have to say, Bill, that we've guessed at the value. I trust that's enough?"

Maybe three to four times what the place was worth, that's all. Six numbers to the left of the decimal point, and the numbers weren't small.

At another time, at another place in his life, he would have asked questions, mainly dealing with where the Junction had come up with cash like this. But this was now, and the withdrawal from his bank account didn't make all that big a lump in his wallet.

He looked up.

Wayman had a fountain pen in his hand.

"Sign here and there," the banker said, pointing, "and the check is yours."

Bill didn't think twice. He didn't read the papers, he just signed where the man indicated, folded the envelope and put it in his pocket. Handshakes all around, a few meaningless words of regret, a farewell to the men in the front room, and he was gone. Hurrying down the street to the passageway, trying not to think of what all that money could do, how it could ensure setting up his own business.

Thinking that it was getting too dark too fast, and there were too many dark places here and not enough sound.

When he reached the car, he touched his pocket to be sure the envelope was still there, then got in, fired the engine, and left.

He drove to the main street and turned east, not looking back, not even checking the rearview mirror. Twilight had arrived, and as he bumped over the rise that marked the railroad tracks, he could see the road ahead, straight and dark, the land to either side, flat and dark.

Topeka, he thought; maybe Wichita. Hell, maybe even all the way to Kansas City.

It really didn't make any difference, as long as he was there and not here.

He grinned as he sped up, laughed as he turned on the radio, shook his head and figured that even if the check was somehow a phony, what counted was that he was gone. Hart Junction was behind him, the rest of the whole damn country straight ahead.

Three miles later he saw them in the middle of the road.

The temptation to laugh and run them down was strong, but he slowed anyway, and stopped when it was obvious they weren't going to move out of the way.

Three of them, in monks' robes with the cowls folded neatly on their backs. Facing him with broad smiles and bright eyes, hands clasped in front of them. He recognized the blonde in the center, who called herself Lark. He was pretty sure the one on the left was Ariel; she'd visited him twice, giving him the literature, trying to make him "see the way." He didn't know the third one, and he didn't give a damn.

He rolled down the window. "Ladies, out of the way, please. I'm in a hurry."

They didn't move.

"Come on, girls, I haven't got all day."

He inched the car forward, but they didn't flinch, didn't shift.

Then Lark's smile widened, and she reached out, and touched the hood.

"Mr. Albright," she said, her tone lightly scolding, "we've been waiting for you. You're late."

FOUR

B e careful what you wish for, Proctor thought
glumly, or it'll step right up and bite you on
the ass.

First was the weather: November had finally returned after the previous few days' respite. Clouds
had moved in overnight on the back of a slow wind,
smearing into an overcast that brought with it a
damp chilly wind and lower temperatures. Color
dulled. The light was grey.

It felt like snow.

It would probably rain.

He sat alone in the living room, thinking, waiting,
knowing and for the moment not caring that half his
lousy mood was self-inflicted.

The room was large, its ceiling high. The wall on
his right was filled with an etched glass-fronted
bookcase; the wall on his left with shelves that held
the TV, stereo, and whatever else he felt like putting
there as he passed by. He faced a three-cushion couch
with a walnut coffee table in front of it, an armchair to
either side. He himself was in a wingback chair, repad-

ded and reupholstered to make it more to his liking, carved walnut trim, lion's-paw feet.

Nothing matched, but it all fit anyway.

Behind the couch, through an archway, was the dining room, not as large but large enough. More often than not the table under the hanging brass lamp was used for spreading files and folders on more than eating. A picture window in the back wall let him see the gloom outside touched with flecks of sunset through the boughs of the mature blue spruce that served as a wall on three sides of his property. No one could see the long, one-story house, and he couldn't see them.

He didn't have to worry about the east side—just beyond the redwood deck that ran most of the house's length was his section of the New Jersey Palisades, a hundred feet or more straight down to the Hudson River.

He shifted, crossed his legs at the ankles, and listened to the soft voices floating out of the hall on the right. He couldn't hear the words, but he could guess:

Don't worry about Proctor, Vivian, he gets into moods now and then and grumbles a lot. He'll get over it. If he doesn't, I'll shoot him.

He almost grinned.

Lana Kelaleha was right, most of the time. He did have moods, and he did grumble a lot. Sometimes it was only the weather, sometimes the bills and payroll that until recently were hard to meet. This time, however, he had cause.

Unless, something told him, you're just behaving like a jerk.

"Lana," he called, "let's get this over with so you can go home."

In his right hand he held Leona Elmdorf's letter; in his left was a flyer she had included with her plea.

Lana came out of the hall, skirted the armchair, sat on the couch, and dropped a pair of folders onto the coffee table. A touch of a finger to the black bangs that covered her brow; an absent push at the straight black hair that drifted above one shoulder. The only light came from the back window and the lamps on the end tables that flanked the couch, the three-way bulbs on their lowest setting, but she didn't move to turn them up.

The breeze became a desultory wind, prowling around the house, igniting drafts that curled at his ankles.

"So," he said from the shadow of the wingback, "what have we got?"

She and a computer team she'd put together herself had spent the last five weeks sifting and searching through literal reams of paper, everything from police reports to credit-card billings, FBI notes and speculations from psychics. All in an attempt to find out what had happened to Taylor Blaine's daughter.

Thirteen years' worth.

She grimaced. "Chico will be retired before we get through it all." She was an exotic mix of Hawaiian and Mexican; her husband, however, was pure Hawaiian, called Chico because she despaired of any mainlanders ever getting his name right.

"I have every confidence in your abilities," he answered with a grin, and a touch of an imitation of Blaine's voice.

"It's going to take a long time," she reminded him, shaking her head. "So far, most of this stuff is redundant, a hundred people going over the same ground a million times, but . . . it's going to take a while just to make sure."

"I told him. He doesn't care. He just wants his daughter back. So . . . what?"

She opened both folders, spread some papers across the table, and nibbled at her lower lip for a few seconds. She had already made a pointed look at the letter in his hand, but that would come later. She knew better than to ask.

"Maude Tackett and Ginger Hong."

He glanced toward the hall and frowned. "Anything we don't already know?"

"Good question, but no, we haven't found anything yet." She touched her bangs again, shifted a page aside. "In June of '84, Celeste Blaine left on a road trip before reporting to college. A few calls for a couple of weeks, then nothing." She looked up. "Maude and Ginger were the two girls with her. They haven't been seen or heard from either. And why is it," she interrupted herself almost angrily, "that Blaine never talks about them?"

"They're not his daughters," he suggested.

"They're somebody's daughters," she snapped. "Somebody has to care about them. Their parents don't have one-tenth the money Blaine does. Certainly not enough to pay for all this, for all this time. Hell, one of them was on welfare at the time, the kid got an academic scholarship." She leaned back, scowling, daring him to argue.

He didn't. The same thing had bothered him since the investigation began, and although Blaine had professed concern, Proctor couldn't help feeling the man considered them an insignificant part of the larger puzzle. He supposed that was natural, given Blaine's youngest child was one of the missing, but he still didn't like it.

"Anyway," she said, "I don't know that there'll be enough information at the end of all this. If I can find something no one else has."

"If it's there," he said gently, "you'll find it."

She shrugged at the compliment, but he could tell by the slight tilt of her head that she was pleased. Although he wasn't a complete computer illiterate, Lana was able to make the damn things get up and dance, and paint the house while they were at it. What he had said was indeed a compliment, but it was also a statement of fact.

"What about you?" she said then, sitting back, nodding at the letter.

A gust batted at the window behind his chair.

He tapped the envelope lightly against his chin. "I've tried calling a couple of times. No luck." A glance at his watch. "I'll try again when I get back home." A reference to the day—Wednesday—and the weekly visit with his mother, in a nursing home.

"And when do you leave? The case, I mean."

"Ten, ten-thirty," a woman's voice answered quietly.

Lana jumped, and laughed as she turned. "Hey, you startled me."

Proctor didn't move.

Leaning against the wall at the hallway entrance was Vivian Chambers, the other reason his mood had gone south.

Not that it was her fault, but she was the handy target. Unfair, perhaps, but that, unfortunately, was the way it was.

The deal with Blaine was simple: Proctor searched for Celeste, except when he took on one of his special cases. When he had called Blaine this morning to inform him he'd be gone for a few days, the old man had asked a favor—that Vivian accompany him. An opportunity, he had explained, to observe how Proctor worked.

Except that she'd been in the office twice a week for the past five weeks, helping Lana and RJ sort through all the papers.

She already knew how Proctor worked.

Proctor had nearly lost his temper, literally bit his tongue to keep from blurting something irretrievable. The fact was, Blaine's arrival had saved Black Oak from a chilling, uncertain future, and Proctor owed him.

He owed him, he knew it, and he hated it.

It wasn't the obligation that he minded. It was Blaine's taking advantage of it so blatantly, and so soon.

"He does care, you know," Vivian said to Lana.

A nod toward the papers. "Those girls. He really does care."

"Funny way to show it," Lana said. Shrugged. Motioned Vivian to sit with her, but Vivian shook her head.

"Been sitting all day. It feels good to stand for a while."

Another gust, and the brass lamp began to swing slowly. Not much, but enough.

Lana grinned at Vivian's expression. "Spooky, huh?"

Vivian nodded uncertainly. "Drafts, right?"

"Well, that's the official story." Lana grinned again at the woman's expression. "You'll get used to it, don't worry."

Vivian didn't answer, but she shifted so she couldn't see the dining room, or the lamp. A hand touched briefly at her long, light brown hair, drifted to her lightly freckled cheek, settled at her waist.

The wind again, and the distinct patter of rain on the windows.

Lana exaggerated a shiver as she rubbed her upper arms. "Would it be too much trouble, Proctor," she complained, "if maybe now we can get the holes in this place plugged?"

All he said was, "See to it."

She nodded, gathered her folders into a pile, and pushed her hands back through her hair. "While you're gone, I'll get a more detailed time line set up. Places, dates, all that stuff. I think . . ." She hesitated. "I think, soon, it'll be time to get into the field."

He nodded, and one of the table lamps flared and went out.

She rolled her eyes. "Oh, for crying out loud." She grabbed up the folders and rose. "I'll get a new bulb from the—"

"Leave it," he said flatly. "Go on home. It's a nasty night. When I get back we'll see about sending Doc out to talk to those families."

"And Taz?"

He shook his head. Paul Tazaretti was the youngest of Black Oak's investigators, and while traveling with Doc Falcon would be an education, he wanted to keep the young man closer to home. The case Taz was on now would, with luck, be over in a few days; after that, he could help Lana with the paperwork, until Proctor needed him.

Five minutes later, the two women stood under the archway, coats on, umbrellas in hand. Lana reminded him to eat something before he went out, and disappeared into the kitchen.

Vivian didn't move, and he could see her struggling with her temper. "It isn't going to be that bad, you know," she said at last. A slightly deep voice, just shy of husky.

He grunted.

She turned her umbrella over in her hands. "You work alone, I take it. With these . . . special cases, I mean."

"Most of the time, yes."

Lana called from the back door, and Vivian took another step before lifting her shoulders in a silent sigh. "Listen," she said evenly, "when Mr. Blaine asked if I could go along, you agreed. No big deal, I think you said. But it *is* a big deal. Obviously. You mind telling me why?" A frown, a skeptical look. "Good God, Proctor, don't tell me it's because I'm a woman."

He opened his mouth to deny it, but she wouldn't give him the chance.

"From what I've seen," she went on, jerking her head toward the hall and the offices that lined it, "you don't exactly have a lot of cases fraught with danger and intrigue. Unless I'm missing something here."

"I—"

She cut him off with a *don't bother* gesture. "It doesn't make any difference. Whatever it is, I can take care of myself. Believe me, that's not a problem." She didn't raise her voice, and the frown was gone. She could have been talking about the weather. "You don't have to worry."

He leaned forward, bringing his face into what little light was left. Then he held up a finger, and kept his voice as even as hers. "First, I am not worried." A second finger. "Second, what you've seen here in the office doesn't always reflect what goes on in the field." A third finger, and he tapped all three against his chest. "And third, Ms. Chambers . . ." he felt his voice begin to rise, held his breath for a moment and lowered his hand to his lap, stared at the lawn. "You have no idea of what there is out there."

"Maybe not. Maybe I can guess."

He looked at her without raising his head. "No. No, you can't."

Her mouth opened, closed, and finally she said, "Come on, Proctor," without pleading, without complaint. "Give me a break here."

She was right; he knew it; but he couldn't bring the apology out. It was intrusion, and he resented it, and he also knew he would damn well have to get used to it.

A concession, then: he made a face to show her he knew how he was behaving and, at the same time, to ask her for patience.

Adjustments on both sides; she wasn't all that thrilled to be in New Jersey, either.

"I'm gone," Lana called impatiently, and they heard the back door shut.

Vivian hesitated, pulled her lower lip between her teeth, then cleared her throat. "This afternoon, when you were talking about that letter . . ." Her eyes closed for a moment. "I mean, Do you . . . I don't want to be insulting, but do you really believe in those things? The spooky stuff, I mean."

"Do you?"

"No." Emphatically. Then, "Well . . . no."

He didn't smile. He leaned back into the shadows. "Sure you do. Sometimes, anyway. You just won't admit it out loud. People will think you're nuts."

She cocked her head in a *maybe* shrug.

He stared at the brass lamp, still swinging slowly, and though she couldn't see him clearly, she couldn't help but look over her shoulder.

"I could," he told her, "give you the old Horatio speech. More things in heaven and earth, and so on." His left hand moved to rub his cheek softly, slip away and come to rest on the rolled wooden end of his armrest. "But that doesn't convince anyone who doesn't believe. Some people . . . no, most people are Missouri types—show me. And some, maybe most, wouldn't believe even if they did see."

He looked at his hand just as she turned her head back.

"The nature of our beast, you see. Modern Man." A knuckle tapped the wood, just loud enough to be heard.

Slowly.

Steadily.

Until she couldn't help staring at it. Listening to it, the careful steady beat while the rain tapped at the windows front and back.

The brass lamp swayed.

"Footsteps in the dark, on an otherwise quiet street."

After a few seconds he knew she could almost hear the echoes.

"Maybe you look, maybe you don't."

Slow; steady.

"Close or far away, it's hard to tell."

Softer now.

"A little touch of nerves, a little touch of fear, a little touch of hey, there's really nothing there."

Fading. And slowing. Until the tapping finally stopped.

"Finally, despite everything you've been telling yourself, you can't help it—you look. You don't want to, but you look."

She waited, said at last, "And?"

"There's no one back there, of course. The street is still empty. Still dark. Nothing back there at all."

He watched her until she met his gaze, and her left hand moved unconsciously to close her coat at the neck.

"But there *were* footsteps," she said, not quite a question.

"Oh, yes. There were." He tapped the wood. "There are always footsteps."

She made to speak, shook her head, and left. But not without looking at the brass lamp one more time.

He waited until the door closed, until he heard her car back out of the driveway. Then he put the flyer he'd been holding into his lap and opened it. Nothing elaborate; no special type or color. *Morning Star* across the top, *Peace* and *Understanding* under each other in the center; *All Are Welcome* across the bottom, flanked by a pair of well-drawn wings.

Leona Elmdorf had circled one of the wings harshly several times with a dark pen, and had drawn an arrow to the margin. When he turned the paper over, there was another note:

These aren't angels' wings, Mr. Proctor, don't be fooled. You only hear them at night.

FIVE

Although flying was Vivian's least favorite mode of travel, she saw nothing odd about preferring Blaine's private jet to the larger airliners. For one thing, it flew closer to the ground—and she was well aware of how ridiculous that reason was; for another, it felt more like a luxury suite than a plane. Its size and appointments were such that, except for the occasional shudder and shimmy, she barely realized she was flying at all.

So far the ride had been a smooth one, and Proctor was up front in the main cabin, dozing in one of the wide, soft leather seats. Not much had been said since she'd picked him up that morning, but she had known even the night before that she wasn't the true reason his mood had been foul.

She was a symptom, which was why she sat in the bedroom now, waiting for Blaine to pick up the phone. When he did, and the pleasantries were dispensed with, she said, "You've made a big mistake, Mr. Blaine, and as soon as we get back, you're going to have to fix it."

Faint static crackled through the transmission.

Finally he said, "I don't understand, Chambers. What have I done?"

"Me." Knowing him as well as she did, she could see him in his Connecticut home's office, scowling his puzzlement, fussing with the tiny brass globe he kept on his desk. "Me," she repeated. "Here. With Proctor."

He chuckled. "Why, Miss Chambers, don't tell me he's . . . whatever they call it these days when a man—"

"You know that's not it," she interrupted. "You know what I mean. You're going to lose him, Mr. Blaine, if you're not careful."

It was a gamble, talking to him like this, but she knew she had earned the right. And she also knew, unlike some others she had seen come and go, that she wouldn't be made to pay because she did it so rarely. Because he trusted her so completely.

He cleared his throat several times. Now he'd be spinning the globe so fast there was a danger it might topple off its marble base. "I only want to make sure—"

"I know," she interrupted. "I know, Mr. Blaine, and I agree with you. But you shouldn't have asked for the favor in the first place." She smiled at the carpeted deck. "Your favors, if I may say so, sound an awful lot like suggestions, and you have to admit that your suggestions are rather . . . forceful."

"I see."

"He's already in your debt, and he doesn't care for it. He accepts it, but it doesn't make him happy."

"He's a proud man."

"Yes," she said. "He is."

"Perhaps . . . perhaps I should have phrased it differently."

"I think you're right."

"He would have made the suggestion himself, wouldn't he. Eventually."

She nodded. "He would have, yes. He still wouldn't like it much, but Mr. Blaine, the way it is now, I don't think he believes you fully trust him."

Static whispered in the silence. She could almost hear the globe rattling.

"My God, Chambers."

She said nothing.

The globe would be still now, and he'd be staring at it as if it were a crystal ball.

"When you get back," he said. "As soon as you get back, I'll see to it."

"Thank you, sir."

"And in the meantime, take care of him."

"Yes, sir, I'll do my best."

"And one more thing."

"Sir?"

"What, exactly, are you after out there? What could possibly interest him in Kansas?"

She hesitated before saying, "Footsteps, Mr. Blaine. Footsteps."

*   *   *

She took the seat in front of Proctor, considered releasing its latch and turning it around to face him, and changed her mind. That was too formal. She wanted his confidence, not a reminder that she worked for Blaine first. So she waited a few moments, then knelt on the seat, folding her arms over the back to watch him.

The one thing she hadn't told Blaine in any of her in-person reports was that Proctor bothered her. No; he unsettled her. The way he kept to the shadows even when there were no shadows to hide him; the way he looked at her—not the appreciative looks, but the ones that made her feel as if . . . as if he were a cat, seeing things no one else could, even when they looked; the way his voice, which wasn't deep at all, sometimes sounded as if it had echoes.

Still, not a bad-looking guy. A little world-weary, his face touched with lines that sometimes made him older than his age, the way he seldom smiled with his whole mouth, just a lopsided one now and then.

"So," Proctor said quietly without opening his eyes, "what did the old man say?"

She started. "You listened?"

"Didn't have to." That one-sided smile. "You've been itching to call him since we took off."

"Business," she answered flatly.

"Good." One eye opened; the smile remained. "So how's business?"

"Fine."

"Good."

She lowered her chin to her arms. "You know, Proctor, you can be damn annoying sometimes."

"So Lana tells me."

She watched the eye close, the smile fade.

It wasn't a dismissal; he was listening.

"When we get there," she began, and stopped. This was dangerous ground, and she didn't want to make him mad. "I mean, I want to understand something. About this case you're on, the one we're going to."

"Sure."

"I read the letter, I saw the flyer. But there were other letters too."

His expression was impassive.

"Why? I mean, I wasn't there when you decided, so . . . why this one?"

She had been at his office often enough to know that no one was ever there when those particular letters were read. No one but Lana, and even she only kept track of his reactions so she could write the so-sorry letters afterward if he chose not to do it himself.

"I don't know," he answered. "It just happens."

"Are you . . . are you ever wrong?"

His eyes opened. "Oh, sure. Sometimes I make a damn fool of myself."

"And other times?"

"Other times, I don't."

She shifted, rubbing her chin lightly across one wrist. "So what are you looking for, Proctor? Why are these cases so important?"

He looked out the window; he didn't answer.

*   *   *

"Tell me something," she said.

"Like what?"

She shrugged. "I don't know. Anything."

The smile returned. "Ms. Chambers, are you trying to understand me or something?"

She smiled back, and shrugged again, and listened as he told her some truly outrageous stories of some of the frauds and scams Black Oak had exposed. Of how those squirrels she had seen around the house were very nearly pets, as long as he kept feeding them, which he did since, if nothing else, they drove Lana and RJ nuts.

In turn, she told him of how she had risen through the ranks of *Hogan & Blaine*, the parent company. Of how Blaine had noticed her early on and had encouraged her, but relied on her to open her own doors. Of how her ex-husband had left her some time ago, not for another woman but because Vivian had turned out to be the more successful of the two. Of how, without specifics, she had once saved Blaine's life, and had been lifted into that inner circle, responsible to no one but the Old Man. Aside from his remaining children, Franklin and Alicia, there was, she intimated, no one he trusted more.

"So," he said, "you're kind of a . . . what?"

"Yes," she answered simply, and when the pilot's voice announced touchdown within the hour, she blinked in surprise, laughed mild embarrassment, and apologized for monopolizing the conversation.

"It's okay," he said graciously. "I didn't mind at all."

She turned her head slightly without shifting her gaze, the look an accusation. "You did that deliberately."

"It's a gift," he answered blithely.

No, she thought, but it's one hell of a talent.

One hand fussed absently with her hair, pulling it back, letting it go, until she realized he was watching.

That he had seen her left ear. What was left of it.

But all he said was, "I guess you don't wear a ponytail very much."

"Sometimes." She kept her gaze on the window, on the clouds that had turned white and insubstantial, the storm now behind them. "It all depends on who I'm with. Where I am. My mood."

He nodded.

"Maybe I'll tell you about it someday."

"Whatever."

She looked at him a moment longer, then nodded, turned, and sat, fastening her seat belt as she decided that Proctor was somehow . . . uncommon, in a way she couldn't yet understand except to know that whatever it was, it made her uneasy.

The landing was smooth, no fuss, no bother. No one met them at the hangar, but the car was there, and she wasn't at all surprised when he took the driver's side without asking. He was anxious to get going, get back in control, get where they were going as fast as he could.

That was fine with her.

So was the quick laugh when they left the ranch and he said, "Which way?" and she pointed east, down an impossibly straight two-lane road.

"Like the desert," he said a few minutes later.

"What do you mean?"

He pointed at the plains that spread away from them in all directions. A low rise once in a while to break up the flat terrain, a narrow dry creek bed here and there, but otherwise without landmarks. No trees, no houses, no hills. "I'll bet if you decide to go for a walk and get too far off the road along here, you'd get lost real easy."

The sun was behind them.

They drove toward the dark.

He was right, she thought. Start wandering around out there, who knows where you'd end up.

The notion made her uncomfortable. So did the sky, a deepening blue as the sun westered. There was too much of it. It made her feel as small as the car would look from the plane they'd just taken. And the horizon was too far away, at the end of the world.

He asked if she knew anything about Hart Junction, but all she could tell him was that it only showed up on detailed maps, and not on all of them. "Barely a dot," she said.

He grunted.

"What do you know about this Morning Star?" she asked in return.

"Nothing. Never heard of it."

"You think it's a cult?"

He shrugged. "I don't know. Maybe."

"I didn't know you dealt with cults, too."

"I'm not a deprogrammer, if that's what you're asking. Sometimes they come up during an investigation, that's all." Then he leaned forward, squinting. "Boy, you'd think you'd be able to see something out here, huh?" He shook his head. "A church steeple or something. God knows, you can see far enough."

Too far, she thought.

The shadow of a cloud rippled across the road.

She looked behind them and saw more clouds, perhaps another storm, massing on the horizon, drawing the sun down.

"No farms, either," he said a while later, after they had passed a buckshot-pocked sign that welcomed them to Kansas. "No ranches that I can tell. What the hell do people do out here?"

"We'll find out soon enough," she answered, pointing. "There it is."

The roofline break in the horizon had, she realized, been there for the past several miles, but she hadn't focused on it. Now, as he sped up a little, she noticed that the road ran straight through the center of town, that there didn't seem to be too many blocks on either side of the main street, and what few trees there were had been stripped of their leaves, their branches like claw marks on the sky.

She blinked and looked at Proctor, as if he had

been the reason for that image. For the abrupt sense of isolation.

What *are* you? she wondered, and wasn't at all sure she really wanted to know. Uncommon, and something more.

The car slowed as Hart Junction began to separate itself into individual buildings, the western edges catching the last of the light.

Less than a mile, and he stopped.

Vivian wished there were a map she could look at, or a page of directions to make sure they were in the right place. But all she could do was stare, her lips twitching toward a smile.

"Wow," she whispered.

And Proctor said, "I'll be damned."

SIX

He slowed the car to a walking pace, not sure what his reaction should be. Disbelief, for certain; a nervous laugh for the incongruity.

Alice and her rabbit hole, he decided, have nothing on us now.

The broad sidewalks were greying wood, and raised several inches above the ground; the buildings were wood, beaten colorless by the weather; hitching posts here and there where curbs and parking meters should have been, along a street half again as wide as the road that fed in and out of it; storefronts with large display windows, faded large lettering, and no neon at all. No streetlamps. No telephone poles.

The side streets little more than alleys, barely wide enough for a single car, and unpaved.

A general store with a dress dummy in the window, a mercantile, a barbershop with a striped pole fixed to the wall beside the entrance; the Gold Star Saloon on the left at the second intersection, complete with batwing doors and a window he half expected to be shattered by a drunk tossed out in a barroom brawl; the narrow front of a sheriff's office, a wood chair beside the door, a spittoon beside the chair; an unnamed shop two doors up, next to the barred windows of the First Junction Bank; a newspaper office whose window announced it the home of the *Junction Gazette*. Another saloon, the Diamond Sal, on the right, its entrance angled to face the alley intersection, a railed balcony that wound around the corner. An undertaker's parlor with a coffin in the window. At the end of the last block, a feed store and stable.

A hundred yards farther on, maybe more, and tracks crossed the tarmac on a slight rise, passing in front of a small depot, its back to the town.

Beyond that the plains returned, unbroken and flat. Slipping into the dark.

Once past the feed store, he turned the car around, lifted his hands in a helpless *I don't get it* gesture and stopped in the middle of the road without switching off the ignition. Without a word he got out, catching his breath at the unexpected chill, and looked back up Main Street, squinting against the setting sun.

The opening of Vivian's door was gunshot loud.

She spoke in a whisper: "If Jesse James comes out of that bank, Proctor, I'm pretty sure I'm going to scream."

He didn't laugh, didn't scowl; he knew exactly how she felt.

Hart Junction was a Western town straight out of the movies, lifted right off the television screen. Exchange the blacktop with dirt, throw in some tumbleweeds and a kid with a melancholy harmonica sitting on an overturned barrel someplace, and the time-travel illusion would be complete.

He shivered a little and rolled his shoulders, reached into the backseat and pulled out his denim jacket. As he slipped it on, he listened, half-expecting to hear the snort of horses, the thin-metal ring of spurs, a tinny piano, the roll of a wagon's wheels.

He heard nothing.

Nothing at all but the faint sigh of a barely felt breeze.

"Where is everybody?" Vivian asked, still whispering.

No traffic, no pedestrians, no lights.

Just the breeze.

He motioned her back into the car and, with his door still open, let the idle drift it off to one side, braking in front of the closed stable doors. When he shut the engine down, the silence was complete.

And when Jesse James stepped out of the bank, he almost choked.

A man with a barely contained stomach paused on the sidewalk outside the bank entrance, peering nervously eastward as he buttoned his topcoat, slipped on his leather gloves. His face was flushed, his dark hair so stiff and gleaming it almost seemed lacquered.

"Jesse," Vivian said wryly, "seems to have gone to pot."

A moment later two women left the Gold Star,

bundled in overcoats, chattering softly to each other as they took the single step down to one of the side streets and disappeared. A man in a plaid flannel shirt, bib coveralls, and a baseball cap pushed back on his head left the Diamond Sal and crossed up and over to the other saloon, quickly followed by two others, hands deep in their pockets, heading in the same direction.

It was like a room full of people, Proctor thought. Eventually nobody speaks, nobody moves. A natural lull that seems a crime to disturb. Sooner or later, however, somebody does, but until then . . . nobody speaks, nobody moves.

He slid out slowly, thinking it odd that none of the people had looked in his direction. Surely standing by the only car within sight would warrant some attention, even from the little kid who raced back and forth across the street up near the far end. A sharp shout, and the boy stopped abruptly, lowered his head and trudged around the corner.

Vivian left the car then, shrugging into a mid-thigh, light leather coat with a broad collar she pulled up with one hand. When he looked at her over the roof of the car, she shrugged, then pointed quickly with her chin.

The feed-store door opened, the faint sound of a bell inside, and a short scrawny man in jeans, metal-tip boots, and a long-johns red top stood on the threshold, scratching hard at his white-spotted beard.

"Excuse me," Proctor said.

The man took his time looking them over. Then he nodded.

"Can you tell me where Leona Elmdorf lives, please?"

"Maybe." The man's hand went into his pockets. "You one of them?"

Proctor leaned a forearm on the car roof, didn't smile, only stared. "Them who?"

The man sniffed, looked up the street for a few seconds before looking back. "If you ain't one of them, who the hell are you?"

Proctor caught the scent of woodsmoke on the breeze, mingling with the unmistakable scent of the stable beside him.

"Personal business," he answered at last.

The man nodded, sniffed again, leaned against the jamb and, unexpectedly, grinned. Instantly, the years Proctor had given him were gone—early forties, no more; it was the beard and its white that had added the age. "Oh yeah," he said, "you must be that Proctor guy, right?"

Proctor felt Vivian stiffen, but he didn't look. He watched the little boy run back into the street, this time followed by a woman in full pursuit. They were too far away, but he thought she might be laughing.

"Leb," the man said, seemingly unperturbed by Proctor's refusal to answer. "Leb Coster. Real name is Lebanon, because my mother was nuts, and bigger than my old man."

"A Bible thing, maybe?" Vivian asked.

He looked at her directly for the first time, and

shrugged an eyebrow. "I don't know. Like I said, she was nuts."

"So what's going on here, Leb?"

Coster pulled a pinch of red material away from his chest, let it snap back. "Not my place to say, Miss Leona's the one."

"Who's the 'them' you thought we were?"

Coster pushed away from the jamb. "Look folks, it's getting on to be suppertime, and it's gonna be dark soon." He checked the sun, already touching the west-end rooftops, balancing above the clouds. "I gotta close up, go home. Leona, she lives up that way, on the corner," and he pointed north. "Can't miss her place, believe me, you won't need no address."

He nodded to her, nodded to Proctor, returned inside and closed the door. Firmly.

Vivian rapped an impatient fingertip on the roof. "Hey, what's the matter with you? He asked you a question, and you didn't answer."

Slowly he turned until he could rest both forearms on the roof. "Sometimes," he said carefully, "it pays not to talk. Sometimes it pays not to ask questions." He glanced up the street, listening to the high-pitched laughter of the unseen little boy. "Silences, Vivian. Most people don't like silences. Sooner or later, they want to fill it. They talk. Once in a while they say something they don't mean to say." He cocked his head, watching a woman leave a shop and duck into the Gold Star Saloon. When he looked back, he smiled. Almost. "Besides, he already knew who I was."

She looked at him a long time before she said, "I think I've just been spanked." No rancor; just filing it away.

He didn't respond, just nodded her into the car and took stock of his appetite. It was just after five, and a meal would go a long way toward taking the edge off his nerves. And his temper. He shouldn't have chided her like that, no matter that it was done lightly. Her job wasn't his job, and he couldn't expect her to fall into the role without making mistakes.

But despite all her efforts to be friendly, and non-threatening, it still rankled that she was here, and the decision hadn't been his.

The nerves, though, were something else. It was nothing Coster had said, nor was it the lack of pedestrians on the street. It was the little boy—his laughter.

In a small town like this, surely no more than a few hundred people from the look of it, sidewalk conversations were the norm, not the exception. Yet save for the two women who'd gone into the alley, not one of the people he had seen had paused long enough to speak to anyone else. The banker had obviously seen the men leaving the saloon, but he'd only gone into the Gold Star, not a wave, not a nod, not a single acknowledgment of any kind; the two men leaving the Diamond Sal had hustled to catch up to the man who had gone ahead, but they hadn't called out to him, hadn't asked him to wait up. A small woman leaving a shop two blocks up had passed another woman, and neither had looked up.

The only sound, sharp in the cold early-evening air, had been the laughter.

He waited a few more seconds, watched a few more people leave shops and what he assumed were offices, and either make their way into the Gold Star or down into the alleys. None came toward the car. None looked at the car.

But he knew they had seen him, every one of them.

As he turned the car north, clouds and rooftops finally took the sun, and what little light remained turned sepia. The scrub and sparse grass between the town and the tracks seemed thicker, more solid; the breeze quickened and blew dust across the blacktop.

"How did he know who you were?" Vivian asked, as he drove slowly along the street.

"Small town, I guess. Leona tells someone, someone tells someone else, word gets around."

"He didn't seem too pleased."

"Yeah. I noticed."

The illusion of the Old West was maintained down the side street—weathered walls, a loading platform in front of two large doors but no sign to indicate what they were used for, hitching posts again. The only contemporary concession was the lights he spotted up near the eaves—single bulbs tucked under metal hoods painted to look like wood. He suspected there were others on Main Street as well.

Nighttime, here, wouldn't be as dark as he'd thought.

When they passed the first intersection, he saw the houses clearly for the first time—regular homes, as he had noted from the highway, close together, separated by fencing of all kinds, small yards in front and large ones in back. Most of those he could see through the spotty twilight were two stories and clapboard; the light wasn't strong enough to see if they were all well kept. Curbside trees that blended with the darkening sky. Cars in driveways, a few pickups, and one large RV.

No sidewalks. Only a band of worn grass with a path worn down the center.

The blacktop was pitted here and there, a perfunctory attempt to fill in a pothole. Weeds poked through cracks. Large patches at the edges worn away to the dirt beneath.

Vivian leaned forward to look across him, leather coat creaking. "Not many people home."

Hardly any lights, most of them muted by shades or curtains.

When they reached the third block she said, "Well, Mr. Coster wasn't kidding, was he."

He parked in front of the house on the northeast corner. It was two stories, low and narrow, a barely straight chimney, a wraparound porch, a gap-tooth hedge that hadn't been trimmed in weeks. A large tree to the left, branches heavy and bare and scraping at the porch roof; a smaller evergreen to the right, most of its needles gone.

Ordinary enough, except for the front yard.

Leona Elmdorf had scattered an impressive assembly of lawn ornaments that ranged from dwarves and flamingos to a seashell shrine that had a Buddha inside, and a Nativity crèche. Sheep, cows, buffalo, bear, a stag with one antler missing, a lawn jockey near the steps holding the reins of a pink-mottled burro. Flanking the foot of the inlaid-stone front walk were a pair of concrete cobras, hoods flared and fangs bared.

"Amazing," she said, when Proctor joined her at the walk.

The house was dark, save for a small feeble light over the front door.

The streetlamp on the corner hadn't yet flicked on.

He checked the length of the block before moving toward the house, Vivian close to his left shoulder, one step behind. He glanced at her once, but she was too preoccupied for comment, checking the house, the yard, looking back at the street. She wasn't nervous, just alert, and he wondered at that as he climbed to the porch, hunted futilely for a doorbell, then knocked.

"This is weird, Proctor," she said quietly, as he knocked again.

He didn't argue, just shivered when the early-evening breeze slipped down his collar.

Two windows overlooked the porch and front yard, and she peered through each as best she could. "No lights, I don't think," she said.

He knocked harder, nearly pounding, stepped back and waited.

No sound but the soft hiss of blown dirt through dying grass.

"Maybe she's at that saloon," Vivian suggested, hands deep in her pockets, shoulders up against the cold.

He shook his head, reached out and turned the doorknob

"Hey," she whispered; a caution.

The door opened, and he stepped inside quickly. "Miss Elmdorf?" he called. "Miss Elmdorf, it's Ethan Proctor."

The slow creak of a floorboard; the sound of his own breathing.

A step forward when Vivian came in behind him; vague slants of light in a room to his left, a faint glow down the hall he faced, all of it from outside.

"Empty," she said.

He inhaled slowly, and caught a lingering scent of lavender. Inhaled again, and there was polish, not recent but there just the same. More than that, there was dust. Age. A damp overlay from the recent rain.

"No," he corrected softly. "Not empty. Deserted."

SEVEN

Leb Coster leaned back against the long counter in his store, legs crossed at the ankles, telephone receiver at his ear. It was a large room, dimly lit, filled with the smells of sacks of feed and dust and straw. He didn't carry a whole lot these days, what with most of the farms going under, and folks leaving; most of his profit came from boarding horses in the stable, and making sure he kept his eyes open.

"Yes," he said with impatient weariness. "Yes, Ike, I know."

He stared at the floor. It needed sweeping again.

"It's him, he told me so, so what did you want me to do? Take out my gun and shoot him? Then what? Shoot the woman, too?"

He grinned, reached around with his free hand and plucked a toothpick from the counter.

"No, I don't know who she is. Partner, wife, how the hell should I know?"

While he listened to Wayman bitching, he worked the toothpick around his teeth, more from habit than necessity, finally settled it in the corner of his mouth and chewed on it absently.

"Look, all I know is, he's on his way to Leona's. I get the feeling he don't know who *they* are yet. And no, I don't know why he didn't come alone, what do you think I am, a damn mind reader? Jesus, Ike, get hold, huh? There's nothing we can do until we find out what he's up to, how he does what he does." He laughed, more like a wheeze. "Maybe he'll go out there, blow them all away, save us a whole hell of a lot of trouble."

Wayman's anger exploded in his ear, and he winced as he yanked the receiver away.

"A joke," he said angrily. "Jesus, Ike, it was a goddamn joke, okay?"

But he knew exactly how the banker felt. Times like this, it didn't pay to get too cocky. Just when you thought you were going to be all right, *they* showed up, smiling and nodding in those stupid monk clothes. Being sweet, being polite, practically helping little old ladies across the street.

Smiling; nodding. Looking at you with those eyes.

He nodded. "What I'm going to do is, Ike, I'm going to clean up a little here, get myself something to eat, go home, watch a little TV, go to bed, get up, come to work in the morning. Just like I always do."

His eyes narrowed. "No, Ike, I am not going to follow him, okay? I ain't gonna do it. Get someone else. Get Bliss or Zona or somebody. I did my bit, I'm off-duty for the night."

He listened to one more complaint. Then: "Jesus,

fool, look out the window, okay? It's damn near dark. You think I'm going to sneak around after dark? After what happened to—all right, all right, God almighty. Damn, but Albright was smart, you know? Maybe I'll do the same, pack up and—"

He laughed and rolled his eyes.

"Relax, Ike, it ain't gonna happen. I'm here for the duration. You just sit tight, I'm betting they'll be by in a while, you can find out for yourself." A glance at the window. "Ike, it's late. I gotta go."

Without waiting for a response, he dropped the receiver into its cradle beside the cash register, dusted his hands on his jeans, and rubbed a weary hand over his eyes. Despite the conversation, the duration was not something he looked forward to anymore.

If he was smart, if he had half a brain, what he'd do is get on old Otis' nag there in the stable and ride. Anywhere. Any direction. Just as long as he wasn't here anymore.

It was tempting but, as he looked out the window, not tempting enough.

The lights had come on over the doors along the street, under the porch roofs, at each alley corner. Triggered automatically, they let the Junction know when evening was officially here.

As if he couldn't tell just by looking at the sky.

"Damn," he muttered, disgusted at his own cowardice, and went to the door, stepped out and looked east. By full nightfall it would be completely black out there, except for two small lights at the depot, and maybe a soft glow some four miles father on. When he looked in the other direction, he saw several dozen people on the sidewalks, popping in and out of the grocery store and other shops, the Gold Star, the Diamond Sal . . . almost as if nothing were wrong.

But hurrying just the same.

Hurrying to beat the setting sun.

A check of his watch, and a glance at the sky again.

A snort of disgust.

"Jesus, Leb," he muttered, "and you want Ike to calm down?" he rolled his eyes, shook his head, and returned inside.

Locking the door behind him.

Dot stood on the sidewalk outside her store and watched as the lights winked on, the street began to fill, and voices drifted in the cool November air. Down at the far end she spotted Leb Coster peeking out of his door, checking, popping back inside.

She grinned.

He'd always reminded her of a prairie dog. Not because of his looks, but the way he moved—popping everywhere, short bursts of energy that propelled him in spurts. If he wasn't such an idiot, she would have liked him. Almost.

A noise inside, and she turned, moved to the threshold, and said, "Timothy Evan Holland, if you're at those marbles again, I'm gonna have to smack your behind." Not very loud, not very sternly, and the giggle that was her son's response made her grin.

It was hard on him, she knew, being the only little kid in town. Nobody his own age to play with, fight with, make secret plans with. It was also hard because practically everybody knew who he was, which made hiding out, sneaking around, without somebody noticing practically impossible.

So when, like today, he decided to make a little mischief, she let the reins loose a little.

She heard the marbles clicking again.

"Timmy!"

"Ain't doing it, Mom."

"Ain't?"

The store was narrow and deep, three aisles of miscellany from cheap toys to thread to string, some hardware items, some kitchen items, a hundred little things that people suddenly realized they needed in the middle of a chore. It had been her husband's, and when he'd walked out four years ago, it became hers. Not an easy life, not a hard life, but it wasn't the life she had planned for herself.

"Mommy?"

"Show yourself, twerp."

His head popped around the end of the center aisle. Right by the marbles. A big grin with a couple of teeth missing, hair that wouldn't stay combed, clothes that wouldn't stay pressed.

"I'm hungry."

"Me too."

"So when do we eat?"

"One hour, honey. One hour."

He made a face and disappeared, and she turned her back on him, leaning against the jamb, arms folded across her stomach, watching the fading light turn a faint shade of amber. A few waves to a few people. The nightly curse at her absent husband. A check of the street down by Leb's place, and she wondered who the new people were, that man and that woman, wondered if they had anything to do with Morning Star.

She straightened suddenly.

"Holy shit."

"Hey, Mom, that's a bad word. You owe me a quarter."

She blinked, and frowned.

They must be the ones.

Not Morning Star at all. Damn, they must be the ones.

An electric surge of excitement made her shiver, and she couldn't help a smile that had nothing to do with mirth.

Timmy joined her, jabbed her hip with an elbow, and held out an open palm. She dug a quarter from her jeans, but she didn't take her gaze from the car.

Sitting down there at the end of the street, just out of direct reach of the lights, its windshield glowing faintly.

It's them, she decided; it's got to be them.

"Honey," she said, taking her son by the shoulder, "I think we're gonna close a little early tonight."

"Can I see the angels fly?"

She didn't answer, but she knew it wasn't angels that flew over town at night.

And it wouldn't be long before her son figured that out.

The sheriff's office was empty.

In the small front room a plain wood desk sat at an angle in the right-hand corner, facing the door and the front window. A ladder-back chair behind it, nothing on its surface. A door in the back wall was thick and banded in iron, with a small barred window at head height. To the left of the door, on the wall, was a gun case. Empty. Its ammunition drawer open a few inches, and empty as well. In the back were three cells, each with a cot, each with a narrow barred window high on the back wall.

Empty.

Nothing moved but dust when a draft sneaked through, and the slow-crawling shadows born of the traveling sun.

The doors were locked, and no one knew who had the keys. No one claimed to be the Law anymore.

In the Gold Star Saloon Ike Wayman dabbed at his forehead with a folded handkerchief, stared at the telephone that had been brought to his table, and decided that something would have to be done pretty soon about Coster. For all his bravado, it was evident the little man was beginning to crack.

Not that any of them were immune to an occasional attack of nerves or cold feet, but Coster had been worse lately. Albright's up and leaving had clearly shaken him, had shaken his faith. Wayman had a bad feeling the man would buckle under the strain, take his money and bolt. Soon. Too soon.

Worse; unlike Albright, a stolid man who kept things to himself, sooner or later Leb would talk. Sooner or later, a drink and a willing ear, and the little man would talk.

He nodded to himself and sat back in his chair, hands folded across his paunch. He hadn't ordered his meal yet, but there was plenty of time. Eventually those newcomers would wander in, oblivious to the night, and he would take their measure. If he was wrong, they would be dealt with; if he was right, then he would make a phone call, and everything would be back on track. Nothing to worry about.

Except poor old Leb.

Hang in there, old friend, he thought resignedly, picking up a tumbler, taking a sip of ice water; hang in there, you old fool, I don't want you to have to die.

Soft blue light in a large empty room.

No furniture, no carpets, no decorations on the wall. Nothing hanging from the high ceiling. No windows.

In the center of the room, a gleaming black pedestal three feet tall, smooth and round. On top, a simple bell jar. Under the glass, an uneven faceted globe no more than three inches across.

It was amber, and it was untouched by the soft blue light.

The room's only door opened, and a line of five cowled figures filed in, moving about the floor randomly until the tallest gestured impatiently, and they sat cross-legged in a ragged circle, facing the pedestal and the amber, adjusting their dark robes to cover legs and feet.

No one spoke.

No one moved.

The soft blue light, and no shadows on the floor.

The tall one gestured again, a brushing motion that would, in another place, signify dismissal. Here, the soft blue light darkened, and the amber globe brightened.

"He's here," the tall one said. The voice was stern, an accusation of failure.

A figure shifted uneasily. "Others have come, nothing happened with them."

The others nodded, all except the tall one.

A different voice: "Are we in trouble?"

The tall one didn't move, but there was a shrug just the same. "It is too soon. By spring . . . another story, but now it's too soon."

No one spoke.

No one moved.

"His name," said the tall one, "is Ethan Proctor."

"Is that important?"

"The name isn't, the man is."

"When will he be here?"

"Tonight, tomorrow."

"Then we'll convert him," said a voice that held a joking smile.

The tall one's head dipped for a moment, and rose. "No."

No one spoke.

No one moved, until the tall one stood and gestured the others to do the same. They faced each other across the circle, hands clasped and heads bowed in what appeared to be silent prayer. A bare foot shifted on the bare floor and squeaked softly; cloth whispered; a faint wheezing inhalation; a cough not quite trapped in someone's throat.

Five minutes; ten.

There was no signal, but heads lifted and hands unclasped as the tall one stepped back out of the circle.

"Listen carefully. This isn't the same as someone's aunt coming for an unexpected visit, or some state bureaucrat nosing around because of some foolish letter."

The soft blue light began to fade.

"The claim is that this man is different. Whether he is or not, we can't afford to argue, we certainly can't afford to doubt. Not now. Now is too important. Dorothy Holland and her boy must be convinced, immediately. And three or four others, you know who they are. Get it done, now, and this man will not harm us."

The voice softened.

"Smile, my darlings, and do your good work. You are protected, there will be no harm to you, you have seen that. So spread your wings, my darlings, and do your good work."

The tall one's hands clapped once, and the others filed out without looking, without saying a word. When the last one had left, the tall one moved to the doorway, hesitated, and stepped through.

The door closed without a sound.

The soft blue became soft black.

And in the blackness, someone laughed.

Softly.

EIGHT

Proctor flicked a switch on the foyer wall and squinted briefly at the bulbs that flared on dimly, from a tarnished brass sconce in the hall and a lamp in the living room to the left. Oddly, the light seemed to shrink the house, not expand it, and where it didn't reflect in the windows the panes were a solid flat black. He took a step on the fringed runner that ran the length of the hall, called Leona's name again, and slipped his hands into his pockets, frowning thoughtfully as Vivian closed the door behind them.

On the right a staircase led to a second-floor landing, and when she offered to check, he only nodded, not watching as she took the steps one at a time, cautiously, left hand gliding lightly along the banister.

The living room was large, but not heavily furnished. A brick fireplace on the far wall, with narrow windows on either side. A sofa facing the two front windows, three small framed oils over the sofa, two chairs that faced the worn brick hearth. A threadbare carpet in the center of the hardwood floor. On the mantel a ragged row of silver-framed photographs. A single lamp on an end table on the sofa's left. A carpetbag on the floor beside the table, a half dozen knitting needles poking from its open mouth.

Where are you, Leona? he asked. A small table by the living-room archway held a black telephone and an address book wrapped in a rubber band. He passed a hand over it but didn't touch it, instead walked toward the back, reached around the jamb and after a few fumbling seconds switched on the overhead light, encased in a milk-glass globe.

"Come on, Leona," he whispered. "Give me a break here, give me a hint."

The kitchen was anything but modern, and almost everything but the drooping brown-edged plants in the back window was a dull, used white, from the refrigerator to the stove to the chipped metal cupboards above the counters that ran along the right-hand wall. A square pine table with four matching chairs. Tins and canisters on the counters.

He moved to the sink—empty, with dark stains around the mouth of the drain.

He opened the refrigerator—empty, except for a quart of milk, a carton of orange juice, two tins of cat food with clear plastic lids, a head of lettuce browning at the edges, and six bottles of beer. He checked the milk; it was ready to turn. He checked the orange juice; it was tart.

"What's up, Leona?" he whispered. "Where have you gone?" He closed the door and stepped back.

Here, as in the foyer, the smell of dust and neglect.

A wall clock in the shape of a grinning black cat with a pendulum tail was stopped—noon or midnight, it didn't matter, the batteries were dead and no one left to replace them.

In the corner by the refrigerator was a crooked plank door with a simple, black-iron latch. Beyond was a small landing, and when he brushed a palm over a wall switch, a bright bulb burned below. No railing, just narrow stairs he took down to the hard-packed dirt floor. Shelves on the wall opposite, filled with wax-sealed glass jars. Exposed ceiling beams. Swaying cobwebs. An old furnace to the right. The cellar was much smaller than the house above, and he could feel the weight over his head; deadweight.

He shook himself and hurried back to the kitchen. The place was getting to him; not a good sign.

Overhead he could hear muffled creaks as Vivian moved from room to room. No footsteps. He frowned, shrugged, and returned to the living room, where he stood with his back to the front windows and wondered.

On all the windows the shades were halfway up; the dark wine draperies were tied back; the paint on the sills here and there peeled to bare wood. The wallpaper was old, roses and ivy and young shepherdesses with reclining sheep. He could see a sag in the sofa cushion nearest the lamp. On a low coffee table in front of the sofa, scattered magazines and a Sunday newspaper, two weeks old. Antimacassars placed neatly over the backs and arms of the chairs and sofa.

The dust on the tabletops wasn't thick, but he could see it.

An open doorway between the sofa and the hearth led into a dining room. He didn't bother to go in; he could guess, and that was enough.

A slow shake of his head, and he pushed hair away from his brow, then stepped back until he was able to perch on the edge of a windowsill. He looked up and saw tiny cracks in the plaster ceiling, and a discolored oval where a light fixture or ceiling fan had once been. There was no place, neither shelves nor cabinets, for knickknacks, or souvenirs, or trophies of any kind. Just the photographs on the mantel. He walked over and examined them without picking them up—old, very old, and he supposed the one couple he saw were Leona's parents; all the others were of two female children from toddler to teen—Leona, maybe, and her sister. The house behind them wasn't this one.

As he returned to his windowsill perch he couldn't help thinking that no one young had lived in this house for a very long time.

He patted the right side of his coat and felt the letter in there, then cocked his head and listened: Vivian moving around upstairs, the voice of a steady breeze across the mouth of the chimney, a beam creaking. No voices outside, no cars, no animals.

No one young, and no one old.

He stared blindly at the carpet.

Where are you, Leona, and how long have you been gone?

He didn't look up when Vivian came down the stairs, stood in the archway, and said, "Nothing."

"Her clothes?"

"Still there, as far as I can tell. Stuff in the bathroom. There's a spare room, but there's nothing but a bed and an empty closet." She shrugged. "There's a storeroom, but just some old furniture, an empty suitcase, cartons with clothes—put-away things for spring and summer, things like that."

"Dust?"

"All over."

He shook his head, rubbed his face with his left hand. It wasn't yet six, but it felt like midnight. The traveling, the time zones, had begun to weary him, make his thinking fuzzy. He rubbed his face again, and his eyes, and when she asked him how long he thought Leona'd been gone, he gestured at the room.

"Hard to say. This dust makes it look like forever, but I'll bet, out here, a good wind just sifts it through the walls." He straightened, stretched his neck. "A few days, though, I'd guess. At least."

"Why didn't she wait for you?"

"Maybe she didn't have a choice."

As soon as he said it, he pushed away from the sill and faced the window. The last of the twilight was gone; he couldn't see more than a couple of feet onto the porch in the lamplight's glow. And even that was blurred by the ghost of his reflection.

There were no lights in the houses across the way, only one that he could see halfway up the block, and he wondered who was home there, and if they had been checking him through the curtains.

The hooded, corner streetlamp was faint, making a solid wall of the hedge and silhouettes of the plaster figures that sat on the lawn.

If he didn't know better, he'd swear they were watching him.

Waiting for him.

Vivian didn't move. "Now what?"

It didn't take much thought: "Coster knew who I was. A town this small, other people probably do, too." After a last look at the yard, he started for the door. "I suggest we refuel, because I'm starving and I'm getting a headache. The saloon's our best bet from what I saw before. I think that's the local eat-and-gossip place." As he passed her, he grinned. "And while we're there we'll make pests of ourselves."

She stopped him in the foyer. "Do you think something's happened to her?"

He stared down the hall. "I wouldn't know."

She looked at him oddly, as if disappointed he hadn't been able to pick an answer out of the air, but wasn't surprised that he hadn't.

I'm not a magician, you know, he wanted to tell her; *I just know things, that's all*

Instead, he opened the door and went out onto the porch, shivering in the early-evening cold. She stood beside him, scanning the neighborhood. Then, without warning: "Are you armed?"

Startled, he nodded without thinking, patting the

left side of his denim jacket where a holster had been sewn into the fleece lining.

"Okay," she said, and stretched. "It's not that far, you want to walk?"

"Sure."

Down the steps, down the walk, around the corner without speaking. The scuff and scrape of their footsteps. Something small scuttling through the brush far to their left, where the land rose in a low embankment to meet the tracks. Amid the darkened houses a door slammed; it sounded like a gunshot.

Between the corner streetlamps a block of night, a short tunnel that accentuated the sounds of their passing and gave them slight echoes.

She kept to his left, sometimes a pace ahead, sometimes a pace behind. Taking her time. Turning once to walk backward a few steps, ignoring the hair the breeze fluttered across her face.

Suddenly he had it, and he couldn't help a grin, just short of snapping his fingers; when she saw it she said, "What?"

"You're his bodyguard, aren't you."

She blinked, once and slowly, before giving him a slow shrug.

"Be damned."

"You have a problem with that?"

"Nope." But he knew now why Blaine had insisted she come along. It wasn't distrust after all; it was protection of his investment. For a second he bristled—did the man think he couldn't take care of himself?—but the foolishness of it made him smile again.

One of these days he would have to stop being so sensitive, so territorial. On the other hand, it was his territory, and the only people in it were there by his invitation.

You, he told himself, are going to drive yourself nuts if you don't cut it out.

She watched him without expression. "You don't look very pleased." Accusing without belligerence; arms loose but never far from her sides.

He couldn't help picturing her wearing a gun belt, slung low, six-guns with ivory grips, rawhide ties. Actually, considering where they were, that wasn't so far-fetched.

"Don't worry about it," he told her. "It just took me a while to figure it out, that's all."

The last intersection before the main street had no light at all, and the hooded bulbs he had spotted on the walls of the building ahead were neither numerous nor bright enough for comfort. Not all were working either, and the glow from those that were barely reached the ground. He was about to comment on the apparent stingy attitude of the town fathers, when he realized Vivian had stopped a few steps behind him.

They had drifted into the middle of the street, and when he returned to her side, she held up a finger, and said, "Listen."

Despite the streetlamps, the few house lights, and the hour, the dark was overwhelming, swarming with shadows teased into movement by the now-steady breeze. Look too hard and he'd begin to see things that weren't there, so he half closed his eyes and concentrated on the silence.

Too big, he thought; like the land here, even the silence is too big.

He looked to her for a clue, but she shook her head.

And he heard it.

A low rhythmic rustling . . . but not quite.

A muted rhythmic snapping . . . but not quite.

It took a moment before he recognized that what he heard was the hushed steady beat of slow-moving wings.

Automatically he looked up, at more stars than he remembered ever being in the sky. With his hands at the sides of his eyes to mute the effect of the light behind him he stared at the dark. Listening. Swiveling his head slowly from side to side, trying to pinpoint the location.

"Bats?" she whispered, staring at the open prairie east of town.

He shook his head; he didn't think so.

Unless they were the biggest damn bats in the world.

Circling slowly overhead, as far as he could tell. Fading, then louder, and fading again. Every so often the stars flickered as something passed over them, too quickly to form an image, no real telling how high or low they were.

Dark wings, circling, and keeping out of range of his vision, and the lights.

He supposed there must be nighthawks of some

kind out here, or owls, maybe even golden eagles, but he didn't know for sure. Whatever they were, they didn't utter a sound.

Circling, nothing more.

He backed up a step, and Vivian backed up with him, her left hand slipping into the low pocket of her coat.

Like the figurines on Leona's lawn then, he had the feeling those birds weren't on the hunt; they were watching him. Checking him out. Ludicrous, maybe, but he couldn't help it—they were up there in the dark, checking him out.

"I think," he said, and stopped.

They were gone.

A few seconds later he lifted a hand in a *beats me* gesture and turned around.

Vivian said, "Oh."

At the east end of the main street, where it slipped from light to haze just before the depot, four figures stood in the road. They wore monks' robes, their hands tucked into large loose sleeves, tasseled rope girdles tied around their waists.

He was tired, and he was hungry, and the light wasn't all that good, but Proctor couldn't help thinking that if he had turned around just a moment sooner he would have seen their cowls settling carefully onto their backs.

Like wings.

NINE

Vivian moved toward the intersection first, left hand still tucked in her coat pocket. Proctor followed in his own good time, hands in his jeans pockets, thumbs out, watching but not staring at the robed figures as they too moved forward. Four abreast, shoulders almost touching.

It didn't take long to realize they were all women.

Most of the hooded lights along the main street were either not working, too dim, or tucked under porches and blocked by posts. Not nearly enough illumination to see anything without straining, and the windows of the feed store and its neighbors across the street were dark.

Vivian shifted behind him to his right when they reached the end of the raised wooden sidewalk, leaving him to nod a greeting to the others.

"Good evening," said the woman in the center. Taller than her companions, long white hair and pale skin, a pleasant smile that did not expose her teeth.

"Evening."

The smile broadened. "Are you at peace?"

He smiled back. "Morning Star."

"Ah." A slight tilt of her head. Her companions smiled, but shyly as they arranged themselves behind her. "You know us then?"

"I've heard, that's all."

"You're new." She bowed her head, looked out from behind a breeze-blown screen of pale white. "I am Ariel." She nodded to a short-cropped blonde. "This is Lark." To a black woman whose scalp was shaven—"Robin." To a brunette with bangs and curls—"Tie."

Proctor moved around the sidewalk to the hitching post and leaned a hip against it. "Short for Titania, right?"

The brunette giggled, and Ariel nodded a compliment, turning her head to let the breeze take the hair from her eyes. "Very good, sir."

"Birds and fairies," he answered solemnly, without mockery. "But a lucky guess, anyway."

The woman gestured—long fingers, pale hand—up the street. "Visiting friends, or just passing through, as they say around here."

He pushed at a stone with his right foot. "Yes."

Vivian stepped up to the sidewalk and leaned a shoulder against the post. He didn't look at her, but he could sense the struggle between restraint and a hundred questions.

"But again," Ariel said, hand tucked back into her sleeves, "are you at peace?"

He looked straight at her. "Are you?"

"Oh, always," she answered without hesitation,

without blinking, without taking offense. "I wouldn't be here otherwise."

"Proselytizing."

She shook her head as though scolding him because he ought to know better. "Visiting. Helping where we can. Lending a hand." A slight shrug. "Some join us, some do not." Another shrug; nothing more to say. The smile returned. "You should visit us, the both of you." The hand pointed west, down the road. "We give it no name ourselves, but around here they call it the old Coglin ranch." She laughed silently. "We could be here a hundred years, I think, and they would still call it the old Coglin ranch."

"Small towns are like that."

"So they are. So they are."

"Will you come?" Robin asked, her voice high-pitched. "It's very nice."

"You know," he said, "I think I probably will." He pushed away from the hitching post and patted his stomach. "But right now I'm starving and need to be fed." He swung up onto the sidewalk, forcing Vivian to step aside. "Maybe tomorrow. In the morning."

Ariel's smile slipped. "There's not much to see during the day."

He glanced at Vivian. "That's okay. If you're not there, I'll talk to Vera." He touched his stomach again. "Vera Elmdorf, right? Leona's sister."

Ariel didn't answer, and the others drifted away without a good night, heads down, gliding south past the feed store, and finally out of the light.

"Our work," she said; and strands of her hair danced and twisted.

A polite wave and a farewell smile, and Proctor started up the street. He didn't know how long the woman watched his back, but when at last he glanced over his shoulder, she was gone.

"Damn," Vivian said. "You always meet weird people like that when you're on the road?"

He didn't answer.

He was too busy listening for the hush of those dark wings.

The horse wasn't much to look at. A little on the mangy side, a distinct sway along the spine, and long past being able to even think about a gallop. Otis didn't mind, though. She was a good old girl, had been with him since forever, and he wasn't about to do anything to hasten her demise.

They rode eastward across the plains, walking mostly, although with the sun already down, he supposed he ought to hurry it up a little, but the Junction was only a mile away, give or take, and he didn't think he'd have to worry.

He grunted then, and the mare twitched her ears.

"It's all right," he said softly, patting her thin neck. "Just thinking, that's all."

The animal snorted, tossed her head, and moved on, a little more quickly as she sensed home closing in.

He smiled and let her go, reins in his gloved right hand, left hand resting on his thigh. He knew how she felt. They had been out for a couple of hours, going nowhere in particular, just away that's all. But the stars had already made their presence known, and the sliver of a moon was so achingly pale it seemed transparent.

In the old days, he would have stopped, just so he could see them all, all the stars and the moon.

In the old days the Junction lit its own stars on the ground, houselights and campfires and headlights from cars and trucks.

Tonight, however, like most nights these days, the only stars were in the sky. The town's lights weren't stars at all, just nervous eyes in the dark.

The mare slowed, stopped, and after a moment's waiting Otis realized that she couldn't see very well, didn't know where to put her feet. He sighed for the age of both of them, clucked, and guided her toward the road, reassuring her there were no prairie-dog towns around, no rock holes, no sudden dips or drops.

In the old days she wouldn't have cared; night or day, she had no sense, only wanted to run.

"Well, damn," he muttered.

This was getting ridiculous, all this in the old days stuff. It wasn't like the place was exactly overrun with crime. No one sold drugs on the street corners, there hadn't been a bank robbery in over twenty years, the only fights he knew of were outside the Diamond Sal, drunks who hadn't anything better to do, and when people died it was usually in the comfort of their own beds.

Usually.

"Now there you go again," he said, shaking his head in disgust.

A chill brushed the back of his neck. He shivered, and flipped up the collar of a coat that was nearly as old as the mare. Maybe he was just too old to figure it out, the way people wanted to live these days. His wife, now, she reckoned the new people weren't really doing any harm. They had spruced up the once-deserted Coglin ranch, repaired the outbuildings, put in a new fence along the road, and though they grew their own vegetables they spent a whole lot of money at the local stores, clothes and food and gas for their two cars.

Model citizens; that's what his wife said.

But Merle, she always looked on the bright side, always had. Even when Bill Albright sold out and moved out, she only said he'd be better off in a bigger place, and she was happy for him. She didn't mention all the others who had gone. Friends. Neighbors. Here one day, just a memory the next.

She never, ever mentioned people like Kira Stark, who just up and vanished.

He eased the mare across a shallow depression and up onto the road. Once on the blacktop, he let her move more quickly. Ahead, the Junction's lights seemed bright and sharp; behind him, there was nothing but shimmering black.

Suddenly, a half mile later, the mare twitched her head and whickered softly, and Otis knew he wasn't alone.

*   *   *

Proctor and Vivian paused just inside the Gold Star's batwing doors, letting warmth replace the outside chill.

The room was wide and deep, more than a dozen large round tables scattered haphazardly across the floor. On the left-hand wall was a long plain bar backed by pyramids of bottles and an etched-glass mirror; at the rear, a small stage with a painted pastoral backdrop and red-velvet curtains tied back with silver roping; to the stage's right, a staircase leading to a gallery that ran above the stage. An upright piano next to the stage. Three large chandeliers below the high ceiling, only the center one lit.

The twenty or so people in the room were concentrated near the stage and piano. When no one came to greet or seat him, Proctor moved to his right, to the table in the corner, and sat with his back to the wall, the large front window at his left shoulder. Vivian took the chair to his right, facing the bar. And the entrance.

Almost as soon as they were settled, a woman pushed through a swinging door at the far end of the bar and made her way toward them. She was a large woman with a mass of unnaturally vivid red hair, her plaid shirt and loose slacks protected by a stained and wrinkled white apron. A smile for one customer, a nod to another, and a warning finger shake at a third who said something that made the others laugh.

When she reached their table, she put her hands

on her hips, and said, "Howdy, stranger, new in—"
And abruptly laughed so hard she grabbed the nearest chair and dropped into it, waving an apologetic hand while the other brushed tears from her eyes. "Sorry," she gasped, swallowed hard, and laughed again. Shaking her head. Holding up a hand to beg their patience.

Vivian grinned, then looked away before she started as well.

Proctor waited impassively, and when the woman finally got control of herself, he said, "I thought it was you."

The woman fingered a tissue from between the buttons of her shirt, wiped her eyes, blew her nose, and stuck the tissue into her apron pocket. "My God, it's been so long since I said that, I didn't think I could pull it off with a straight face."

"You didn't," Vivian said, grinning.

"Story of my life," the woman answered, leaning back, fanning herself with one hand. Then she said to Proctor, "What was it, the line or the laugh?"

"You," he answered, finally allowing himself a smile. "I'd know you anywhere, Ms. Paradise." He looked to Vivian, whose grin had become uncertain. "Hazel Paradise. Maybe a zillion Westerns, and the only time she didn't play the owner of the local saloon was when she was the daughter of an itinerant preacher who turned out to be a gambler in disguise."

"No kidding?" Vivian looked from one to the

other as if expecting one of them to let her in on the joke.

"True enough," Hazel admitted, taking a deep breath and blowing it out loudly. "But it's just plain old Hazel Platt now. I haven't seen a camera in . . . God, it must be thirty years and forty pounds ago. And you," she said to Proctor, "are much too young to have seen all those films."

"Television," he answered with a nod to the compliment. "My childhood curse."

Behind her the others had finally begun to pay them some heed; sideways glances, stares over shoulders—everything but outright pointing. He spotted Leb Coster near the piano, scratching through his beard and whispering to a man in a three-piece suit. At the table next to them, a little boy stood and stared, despite a young woman's attempts to make him sit and eat.

"Never met him," Hazel said in answer to a question Proctor hadn't heard. "He was Big Time, honey, and I was strictly B-movie." She winked as she fished a pair of salt and pepper shakers from her apron, placed them on the table and brushed the apron off. "I still own the damn saloon, though. Only now it's burgers and slaw instead of rotgut and beer. Them bottles back there are mostly colored water." She inhaled deeply. "So, what'll it be . . . stranger? Sandwich night tonight. Burgers, grilled cheese, ham, got a little pastrami left over but only if you don't care if your heart explodes in the morning."

She took an order pad from a pocket, and a pencil

from somewhere in the mass of red hair, touched the point of the pencil to her tongue and waited expectantly.

Still acting, Proctor thought then, and told her what he wanted with a wry lopsided smile, nodded at a suggestion of salad and fries on the side, and leaned back until, Vivian's order taken, the woman grabbed the edge of the table and hauled herself smoothly to her feet.

"No fast-food crap," she said as she turned away. "It'll be a few minutes."

A momentary silence.

Vivian unbuttoned her coat and plucked at the light sweater beneath. "Warm in here."

"Keeps out the cold."

"Funny thing," she said, taking stock of the room and the other customers. "Two strangers walk in"— she grinned and sobered within a blink—"and she doesn't ask where we're from, who we are, what we're doing here." She picked up the saltshaker and turned it around in her hands. "Funny thing."

"Not so funny."

She looked at him, set the shaker on the table and spun it like a top. "She already knows."

He nodded.

A handful of customers left, slipping on coats and gloves and hats as they said their good-byes. Avoiding eye contact with him. Hurrying out into the cold.

"They all know," she said, and spun the shaker again, not spilling a grain.

He listened to the rattle of heavy glass against wood until she stopped it with her thumb and nudged it to one side.

Coster left with a friend, nodding a curt greeting before they pushed through the doors.

Proctor glanced up at the gallery and wondered what was behind the three doors he saw up there. Maybe nothing, if they were as much a facade as he was being treated to down here.

An old man hobbled in, bundled as if he'd just left a blizzard, his cane loud on the floorboards as he made his slow way toward an empty table near the staircase. A few voices raised in greeting. Some nods; a halfhearted wave. The little boy ran over and began to talk to him earnestly.

Soon after, a couple came in, arm in arm, heads close together, whispering, the woman giggling into a palm. They took a center table, their backs to the door.

Hazel returned with their meals, joked about the calories as she patted her ample hips, marveled at Vivian's figure, and left to take care of the newcomers, all without seeming to draw a single breath.

"We should have asked her about Leona," Vivian said, picking up one of her two hamburgers, thick with everything Hazel had recommended go on it.

"Later." His stomach growled, demanding attention. He hitched his chair closer to the table, lowered his voice, and said, "Maybe by then they'll figure out what they're going to tell us."

*   *   *

The old mare moved hesitantly in the dark, swerving back and forth across the road. She wanted to move faster, but her legs had no strength; one attempt at galloping had made her stumble, down on her knees until she righted herself. Snorting at the burning on her forelegs. Tossing her head as she listened for pursuit. For help. Thick froth bubbling at the corners of her mouth and dripping in long strings to the blacktop. Eyes wide and white. Ears back, tail snapping. Moving easier because there was no weight on her back, but not fast enough. Heading for the light straight ahead, because she knew that was where the stable was, and food, and warmth. Bucking once, half an effort, to rid her back of the saddle. Nostrils wide, smelling the night, smelling the fear.

Smelling the blood.

TEN

Sated, and pleasantly surprised at how good the simple meal was, Proctor slid his plate away, sat back, and wiped his mouth with a napkin. Hard. To remind him that he hadn't somehow fallen into a dream.

It wouldn't be hard to believe it.

Saloons and hitching posts, a town straight out of old Dodge, and a cast of characters a blind man would recognize. The young mother with her cute rambunctious son, the old codger, the still-flirtatious newly marrieds . . . hell, he wouldn't be surprised if the three-piece suit Coster had been talking to was the parsimonious and greedy town banker. And he certainly couldn't leave out the tough and boisterous owner of the Diamond Sal's rival.

It might have almost been a bizarre kind of fun if he hadn't met Hazel.

In a way, he was sorry it had happened.

A youngster, having grown, should never meet the objects of his youthful dream-lusts. On film they never grew older, or old. They had names like Paradise, not Platt. They always wore soft snug sweaters, or low-cut gowns with pinched waists, velvet chokers, and maybe, once in a while, a flower or gem in their hair. Red lips and exotic eyes. Fluttering fingers and the promise of a kiss like no other. And he wondered for a moment about the others he knew, in Westerns and mysteries and films dotted with dark castles—Ingrid Pitt and Yvette Vickers, Gloria Talbott and Lupe Velez, and the other Hazel in his life, Hazel Court.

He lowered his head and closed his eyes, briefly brushed by a melancholy that made him shake his head.

Then Vivian said, "Company," and the near dream was over.

Merle Dugan was a fusser and proud of it. If she didn't fuss, nothing would ever get done around the house. If she didn't fuss, Otis would spend half his time pampering that foolish old horse, and the other half sitting in front of the TV, yelling at the screen. It didn't matter if it was a football game or the news; he let his feelings be known.

And wouldn't he be shocked if one of these days it decided to yell back.

She loved him dearly, but sometimes he could be a real chore to handle. Getting old and cranky was his usual laughing excuse. Ornery was much more like it. And he always had been, to one degree or another, since the day she had met him.

Tonight was no exception.

Here it was, going on half past six, and he was still out there, riding around like he was still in those foolish movies instead of sitting down at the table to dinner. Forty years, give or take, and he still couldn't tell when it was time to come home to eat.

She fussed, then, with the table, making sure it was set the way he liked it—or, she thought with a mischievous smile, the way she'd taught him to like it. When she was satisfied, she went into the kitchen and fussed with the stove, checked to be sure the roast wasn't burned yet and the vegetables were all right, then wiped her hands on a towel and hurried into the living room to stare at the overhead light.

The bulb was out, and isn't that always the way it was when you had other things on your mind?

The only bulb in the entire house that she couldn't reach without help, and when it finally goes, the old fool isn't home to fix it.

Hands on comfortably wide hips, she stared at the dark shadow under the cut-glass shade, worrying at her bottom lip while she tried to think of a way to take care of it herself. The stepladder was out of the question; getting the shade off would be too awkward, and she didn't want to fall. The kitchen stool would be too shaky, the hassock not high enough, but she had to do something.

A dark bulb in a house was bad luck.

If it wasn't changed soon, something awful would happen.

She clasped her hands and walked around it, checking it from every angle until her neck began to ache. She reached out a hand, but the distance was too great, unless a miracle happened and she suddenly grew a few feet taller. When she realized she was making herself dizzy, staring up like that, she tapped a finger against her cheek until her eyes widened with a sudden thought, and she wondered if she could dare call that nice Dorothy Holland. She wouldn't mind coming over; she would know what to do.

Self-sufficient was what Dorothy was, ever since her husband left her. Self-sufficient people always knew what to do. And there were plenty of fresh cookies in the tin for that little boy of hers.

"Yes," she said decisively to the empty room. "Exactly what I'll do. Exactly."

A single clap of her hands, a congratulatory smile, a wink, and she went to the table beside Otis' beat-up chair, picked up the receiver . . . and gasped and froze when she looked out the front window.

"Oh, dear."

The sun was gone.

"Oh, dear."

It had started already.

She had fussed and fretted for so long, she had forgotten the time, and now it was too late, she couldn't ask that poor child to come over here now. Still staring at the window, she fumbled the receiver back onto its cradle, clasped her hands again, tightly, and tucked them under her chin. She had to do something; she couldn't let the house live with a dark bulb one minute longer and Otis was late and she could smell the roast beginning to burn and if she didn't think of something soon, she just knew she was going to cry, and Otis hated it when she cried.

He simply hated it.

When the doorbell rang—once, and once again—she jumped and almost laughed aloud because the darling old fool had left his key home again. Just like a man. Just like an ornery, wonderful old man.

The smile that she wore when she opened the door wavered only a moment before she recognized her visitor and realized that miracles really do happen sometimes.

"Oh, come in, dear, come in," she said cheerfully, gratefully. "You shouldn't be out in the dark, you know, but you have no idea how glad I am to see you. Aren't you cold, you poor thing? Aren't you cold?"

The man in the three-piece suit, watch chain on a vest that strained across his paunch, introduced himself as Ike Wayman, president of the local bank and unofficial town mayor. It was all Proctor could do to keep from laughing as he rose to shake the man's hand and wave him into a chair.

"Enjoy your meal, folks?" Wayman asked, carefully folding a black cashmere topcoat across his lap. A polite smile, an amiable tone, and when he passed a manicured hand over his scalp, a small diamond ring that flared in the chandelier light.

"Very nice, thanks." Proctor kept his own tone neutral.

Wayman nodded as if he'd expected no other response. "Hazel does very well with what she has. A remarkable woman." A pause, and he cleared his throat. "So." His smile became expectant, awaiting explanation, as he felt was his due.

"Interesting town here," Vivian said instead.

The banker spread his hands, a modest acknowledgment of an implied compliment. "There aren't too many others like it, that's for sure." He leaned forward, lowered his voice. "Movies, you see."

"I'm sorry?" she said.

He glanced back at the other diners, resettled his topcoat, and cleared his throat softly.

"Back in the mid-forties, it was. Hazel's better at this than I am, but she doesn't like to talk about it much. But back in the forties, a Hollywood director, I don't quite remember his name, he got stuck here when the train jumped the tracks during a nasty winter storm. For whatever reason, he liked it. All this open land, the ranches and farms. Mostly farms, of course. He wanted to know about Indians, did they ever live here, things like that. Cowboys, that kind of thing."

"No kidding. And were there? Cowboys and Indians, I mean."

Evidently not, Proctor figured as the story unfolded. But he didn't interrupt; he let Vivian do the smiling and the wide-eyed prodding since the banker was clearly more taken by her than by him.

As a result of her attention, just short of mockingly, embarrassingly, rapt, the man shifted his weight as if preparing to lay siege to her, and Proctor fought the urge to kick her ankle under the table.

Impressed by the town's friendliness and cooperation, Wayman told her, the Hollywood director returned that spring, brought some people with him, shot a few location scenes without actors, and left. Just when they thought that was that, summer brought an entire company, and when someone overheard a complaint that they would have to travel deep into Colorado either to find or build a supposed typical Western town, or return to the same old dreary backlots in California, hasty meetings were convened, a committee formed, and the next thing the Junction knew its main street had been transformed.

The Junction didn't exactly boom into a movie capital, but the business returned fairly regularly; more so when television began cranking out its own Western tales. Townspeople became extras, bit players, and once in a while snared a major part or two. Apparently there wasn't anyone who wasn't involved, one way or another.

"Then it all died," he said, "and now we look like a museum." A quick smile of regret, a shrug, a sigh. "But we manage. And we have our memories."

As the man talked, more customers left and were replaced by others. Someone fooled with the piano, the sound tinny and just barely in tune.

In the large room, it sounded lonely.

Proctor watched them all as he listened, not really paying attention to the faces, just the way they came and went. The tables at the back of the room emptied and filled, but no one ever came to sit near them, and Hazel never returned to see how they were doing.

"So," Wayman said, placing his palms on the table. His booster story was done; now it was their turn. "To what do we owe this—"

"You don't sell real estate, too, do you?" Vivian asked before he finished.

Wayman laughed silently. "I guess I do go on, don't I? It's a failing of mine. We don't get many strangers around here as a rule." He gestured toward the street. "We're not exactly on the main tourist routes these days, as you can tell."

"Morning Star made it," Proctor said, speaking for the first time since the story began.

Wayman looked momentarily confused. "Well . . . yes." A just-between-us expression: "But they're not really part of what's going on, you understand. Town life, I mean."

"Trouble?"

The banker shook his head quickly. "Good heavens, no." His eyes narrowed slightly. "Is that why you're here?"

"They're funny things sometimes," Proctor said, reaching out to nudge at his plate. "Religious cults, that is." He spoke softly, staring at the remnants of his dinner. "People are afraid they'll come in and steal their children."

"I don't think so," Wayman said, still puzzled. "The only child here is little Timmy Holland." He grunted. "The young ones don't usually stick around once their schooling's done."

Little Timmy, Proctor thought; good Lord, he better not have a mangy dog named Shep.

"We met some of them earlier, you know," Vivian said lightly. "The Morning Star people. They seemed awfully nice."

Wayman slipped his hands under the topcoat. "Well, they do help out once in a while," he admitted grudgingly. "Mostly with the old folks. Do their shopping, help around the yard, things like that." He leaned forward, a confidence in the making. "Kind of strange, however, as you may have gathered. They're all women, you know, but they wear those men's robes. Monks, I think." He shook his head and leaned back. "They're polite, they don't push their religion, and they pretty much keep to themselves."

Vivian spread her hands. "Well, I suppose you can't ask for any more than that."

"No," the man said shortly, irritation at their non-answers beginning to color his voice. He looked at them both, his eyes narrowed again. "Now if you don't mind, I'd like to—"

The doors slapped open noisily, and a large man in a sheepskin coat and Western hat stumbled in, puffing, the cold that followed him turning people's heads. He looked around desperately, finally blurted, "Otis, it's Otis," and ran out again.

ELEVEN

It seemed like an hour, was only a few seconds—no one moved, no one spoke. They only gaped at the door and stared at each other.

Proctor waited.

Then Wayman rose so quickly he tipped his chair over, kicked it aside impatiently as he punched into his coat. "Excuse me," he muttered tersely, and was gone, topcoat tails flapping behind him like a cape.

The noise of his leaving was catalyst enough—before the batwings had stopped swinging, half the men in the room were on their feet, scrambling for the exit as they struggled into their coats and jammed on their hats.

Proctor twisted around toward the window, but the inside light fogged the outside view with too many blurred reflections. All he could see were shadow-figures milling around on the street, surrounding what appeared to be a riderless horse. With a jerk of his head to Vivian, he grabbed his coat and headed for the doors, letting the rest of the customers ease him through.

Once on the sidewalk, he sidestepped quickly to his left, out of the anxious flow, and stood on the edge of the sidewalk, hands deep in his pockets, chin tucked toward his chest.

The lighting here was nearly as vague as it was down near the depot; spots of light, spots of dark, and in the center of the street it seemed like black mist.

Hands were raised, voices competed, and a large man raced up from the Diamond Sal, spinning himself clumsily as he tried to get his coat on; someone shouted a demand for silence, someone else's shout was incoherent and enraged.

"My God," Vivian whispered beside him.

In the midst of the crowd, the horse stood quietly, clearly exhausted, head down, barely able to stand. Saddled, reins dangling from the bridle, it swayed in place, foam dripping from its mouth, its eyes white and wide. Another shout finally brought the noise level down from an agitated roar, leaving the men and women to elbow closer to the horse, and slide away, pale and silent. Through the drifting gaps they created Proctor saw dark gleaming streaks on the saddle and the animal's flanks.

Vivian leaned close, pointing with her chin. "Is that—"

"Yes."

"God, what could do that to a horse?"

"I don't know," he said, "but I don't think it's his."

Gentle hands brushed over the trembling animal's head and mane; the saddle was removed, and after a brief discussion, Leb Coster grabbed the saddle with one hand, the reins with the other, and led the horse down the street toward the stable. He looked over at Proctor, looked away, and moved on.

For a long time the only sound was weary hooves on the blacktop.

Then the man who had sounded the alarm snapped an order, and the group split up, vanishing into the alleys, their voices raised and soon fading.

It didn't take very long to leave the street deserted.

Spots of light; spots of dark.

The push of a slow wind that made some of the lights tremble, some of the shadows shrink and grow.

Proctor watched his breath curl away in the cold, blew on his hands, and tugged briefly at Vivian's sleeve before returning to the saloon.

The room was empty, save for a young man in a long white apron weaving carefully around the tables, a large tray in his hands. Muttering to himself.

Outside, a pickup's engine roared, followed by several others, and the prolonged squeal of tires that couldn't immediately find their traction.

Search party, Proctor figured, and watched the busboy make his way to their table, head cocked to one side, a vacant smile on his lips.

Muttering; still muttering.

Vivian started to say something, but he held up a hand to keep her quiet and walked slowly across the floor.

"Never," the busboy said, picking up the plates and glasses to put on the tray. His hair was straight and dark and short, his angular face pale, dark pouches under his eyes. "Never gonna do it. Never happen, never happen."

Proctor stopped by the window, feeling the cold seep below his collar.

A car roared and backfired up the street, shattering the Western town illusion.

The busboy ignored the commotion. He lifted the tray, set it down, and slid the plates back onto the table as if he were serving, not cleaning. "Never find her, never find her. Waste of time now, never gonna find *him*." He chuckled, a sad hollow sound, and picked up the plates again. Examined them as if he had never seen their like before, before arranging them on the tray a second time, one to each quadrant. "Too late, I ain't lying, too late, too late."

"Maybe not," said Proctor quietly.

Startled, the young man looked over, thick strands of dark hair cutting across his forehead. "Dark," he said, nodding to the window at Proctor's back.

Proctor agreed. "Yeah, I guess it is. But they're all out there anyway, looking."

The busboy nodded, then grinned, baring all his teeth. Too widely, too stiffly, before the grin slipped away into an expression of such intense despair that Proctor almost walked over to grab his shoulder for comfort. "Should've gone," he said miserably.

Proctor pointed a thumb toward the street. "The whole town's out there already, it looks like. I don't know if one more would help."

The door at the far end of the bar swung open, someone back there, listening.

Vivian, hands in her pockets and coat hooked behind her elbows, perched on the edge of the table nearest the entrance. The busboy saw her, blinked furiously, and said, "You married? You have a husband?" He tilted his head toward Proctor, eyebrows raised.

"No," she answered with a smile. "Believe it or not, I'm his bodyguard."

The young man laughed, more a cackle, and slid all the dishes from the tray onto the table. "I was. Married."

"Okay," she said.

Hazel stepped out of the kitchen. Proctor saw but didn't acknowledge her; Vivian didn't turn. Instead, they watched the busboy arranging the dishes again, lifting the tray, putting it down, dishes on the table, dishes back on the tray. At first he thought the man was just slow, but when he turned his back on Vivian to stare dumbly at the chairs, blinking, lips quivering, he knew there was something more at work here.

"Kenny," said Hazel sternly.

The young man straightened and looked over. An uncertain grin, a brief confused frown.

"Come on Kenny, we've got a lot of work back here. Gotta get ready for when they get back. You know how they fuss when they don't get their food."

He stared dumbly at her until she said, more gently, "Come on Kenny, honey."

A shuddering sigh, and he filled the tray again.

Slowly, as if the plates and glasses had suddenly gained a weight he wasn't sure he could handle. "Coming," he said.

"That's okay."

He picked up the saltshaker, poured some into his right hand and tossed it over his left shoulder. Cackled. Sighed. Put the shaker on the tray.

His voice was soft, and filled the room: "Never gonna find him, never, never. Too late, too late, never gonna happen." He hoisted the loaded tray to his left shoulder and looked straight at Proctor. "She left me, you know. All I found was the blood." He looked at Vivian. "I was married once, and now all I have is her blood."

"Kenny!" Hazel snapped. "Now, please."

He didn't hurry, didn't dawdle, and when he finally passed her, she laid a hand on his back to ease him into the next room. She stared at the door until it stopped swinging, then looked back at Proctor, who waited for her to speak and wasn't surprised when she shook her head as if scolding herself and disappeared into the kitchen.

He waited, but she didn't return.

"Proctor."

He walked to the batwing doors, touching Vivian's arm as he passed to ask her to follow. Once outside, he took a slow deep breath and held it. It was much too warm in there; he hadn't realized it before, and he was grateful now for the shock of cold that quickly cleared his head.

Bloodied horses and a modern-day posse; half-empty saloons and flying things much too large to be bats; a missing woman and strange women in robes; a woman who figured in a lot of his adolescent dreams, and a young man who seemed to be living dreams of his own.

He had a feeling, neither good nor bad, that when it all finally made sense, he wasn't going to like it. Assuming, of course, it was going to make any sense at all.

"Proctor," Vivian said, stepping down to the street, "you do realize, don't you, that after all this time nobody has told us a damn thing about anything."

"Yep."

She grabbed the end of the hitching post and tugged at it several times without much force, grunted and stepped back, dusting her hands against her sides. "They didn't even ask about Leona."

He looked into the saloon just as half the lights dimmed. The chairs and tables seemed to shimmer in the light that was left. Ghost furniture, he thought, and immediately told himself to knock it off.

"No, they sure didn't."

"So then . . . what are you going to do?"

He scratched through his hair, slapped most of it back in place, rubbed a finger under his nose, and said, "Well, we could wait for them to get back, see what happened out there. You don't have to be a detective to know it isn't going to be good."

"They could be gone all night."

"Okay, so we can go back inside, talk to Hazel or Kenny."

She snorted. "Oh, right. The way she protected him? We won't even get into the kitchen." She frowned up at him. "Look, you already know what you're going to do, so stop jerking me around, okay? And if you're trying to teach me another lesson, forget it, I'm not interested."

He gave her a half smile—*sure you are*—and jumped down to the street. "You asked me before if I was armed. Are you?"

She just looked at him.

"Okay, then let's go."

"Where?"

"There," he said, pointing to the nearest alley. "We're going to roust a town."

TWELVE

Leb sat on the stable floor, knees drawn to his chest. The double doors were open an inch or two, and a narrow slant of dim light passed his left shoulder and barely reached the facing stall. Absently he scraped his teeth over the nail of his right thumb, while the other hand rubbed the side of his face from temple to jaw. Over and over. Pausing now and then to scratch at his beard or pass hard under his nose to keep from sneezing.

He needed silence.

He needed to think.

The first decision had been laughably easy: no way on God's earth was he going out there tonight. Let Bliss and Wayman and the others make damn fools of themselves, thinking they were going to find Otis out there. They knew they weren't; they had seen the damn horse. And if by some damnable miracle they did, there wouldn't be enough left to bring home in a midget's knapsack.

His hand drifted down to the bottle at his side, gripped the neck, lifted, and waited until he was sure he needed another courage-ounce before bringing it to his lips.

A gulp, a cough, and he put the bottle down.

Ken Stark was lucky. He had gone looking for his dumb wife on his own. Lucky because he'd found her, and his mind had gone south and he barely remembered his own name anymore.

But at least he was still alive. A hell of a lot better than Otis probably was.

He lowered his head as if in prayer, and listened to the old nameless mare stir in her stall. He'd done what he could for the poor old gal, rubbing her down, drying her off, a little water, a little hay, a fresh warm blanket to stop the shivering that made her legs weak. But he had a feeling from the way she'd looked at him while he worked that she wasn't long for this world anymore.

Not after what she'd probably seen.

Damnit, Otis, you dumb shit, what the hell were you doing out there tonight? Still think it's the good old days, you stupid old fool?

He sighed wearily and leaned his head back against the wall, fingers brushing the bottle, caressing it, holding on.

Everything inside him, every ounce of sense he had left, screamed at him to get up off his butt, run like hell home, get into the damn truck and ride the hell away. It didn't make a damn difference what direction it was, as long as it was away. He didn't need any more money; he had enough to take care of himself for the rest of his miserable life. The others wouldn't care. More for them, that's all.

If he stayed, he was going to die.

He knew it; he just knew it.

Just like he knew that that son of a bitch Proctor was going to figure it all out no matter what Wayman claimed, and Leb didn't want to be around when the fire came down.

He looked to the gap between the doors, looked at the light and the dust clinging to the air, pictured the short distance from here to the house just behind the stables . . . and didn't move.

Couldn't move.

He picked up the bottle, took a drink, and began to cry.

Shivering, Vivian stood on the corner and checked the street in either direction. No house lights, no movement. A lone streetlamp a few yards up on the left underscored the darkness by barely lighting its own pole. It was so quiet she was getting spooked by the creak of her own jacket each time she shifted her weight, took a step.

"We'll start here," Proctor told her, pointing to the house on their left.

"And do what?"

"See if anyone's home."

He walked off without further explanation, not even a hint, and she could feel irritation tensing the muscles in her neck as she followed.

This was nuts.

He was nuts.

She hadn't believed he was being literal when he'd said he wanted to roust the town; she had thought that was some kind of Proctor-shorthand for hunting up someone who would answer their questions. Of which she had a few dozen or more. But when he hurried up the walk and pounded on the door, rang the bell, and pounded a few more times, she realized rousting was exactly what he meant.

"No one home," he said unnecessarily. "Let's try next door."

"What are you going to say when someone answers?"

"Won't be a problem."

He was right.

They tried every house to the corner, crossed over and made their way west.

No one home.

Anywhere.

By the time they reached the end of the block her nerves had taken over the irritation. She tried a few doors herself, frustration making her hit them harder than she wanted. She didn't even feel the cold anymore. All she wanted was to find someone behind one of those doors, one of those windows. Anyone; it didn't matter. She'd even be happy if she could get a rise from a dog.

Although there were a handful of house lights on the next block over, there was still no response, and her knuckles had gotten tender. Worse for her impatience, Proctor had refused to allow them to separate so they could cover more ground more quickly. On the one hand, it made it easier to watch his back; on the other, the delay made her want to scream.

She wanted this madness over with.

She wanted explanations, but he kept putting her off.

"Later," had become the most hated word in the language.

She was also unhappy with the way he kept checking the sky, as though he half expected to hear those wing sounds again.

It didn't take very long before she did hear them—when they were on porches, between footsteps, between increasingly harsh breaths. They were everywhere, and though she knew they weren't there at all, she heard them anyway.

After they finished canvassing the second block, he stood beneath a streetlamp no more effective than any of the others, and said, hands on hips, "Two, three more blocks. I don't think we have to do any more."

"Thank you," she said sarcastically.

He flashed her that maddening smile of his, never quite using all his mouth, and suggested they head for the stables. The runt, Leb Coster, had taken the horse in that direction, and if he hadn't gone after the others on the search, Proctor wanted to talk to him before the others returned.

"How do you know he'll give us any information?"

"Oh, he will," Proctor answered, touching her arm, walking away.

"Ah, I get it," she said sourly, keeping at his side. "I play the sweet female admirer again, right? He talks, you listen like you did with that banker, and divine all the answers."

"Not this time." He looked at her, only half-turning his head. "How good are you at intimidation?"

Not half as good as you, she thought, and almost stopped when she realized that it was probably true.

"I do all right." She hoped he hadn't noticed the slight hesitation. "But gosh darn it, Proctor, I left my rubber hose in the car."

"Make do," he told her with a laugh. "Improvise."

A half a block in silence before she said, "How did you know there wouldn't be anyone home?"

"It was a guess," he admitted. "But I wasn't surprised."

"You," she said, "don't guess."

Again that damn smile. "Well, yeah, I do, sometimes. But okay, think about this: we sat in that saloon, restaurant, whatever the hell they call it, for well over an hour. People left and came in through most of that time." He held up a finger. "But never alone, except for that old man, the guy with the cane."

"You have a lousy memory." She jerked a thumb upward. "I wouldn't walk around this place alone at night either."

"Why?" He touched his ear. "We heard something,

we didn't see it. So what was it? And is that what's keeping them traveling in bunches?"

"I don't know, and probably." She kicked at a stone, wincing at the noise it made, rattling across the blacktop. "And that still doesn't tell me why we didn't find anyone home."

"Maybe," he said, "it's because I'm getting a strong feeling you and I have been conned."

Timmy Holland stood at his bedroom window, looking out at the prairie. In the far distance he could see tiny explosions of white as flashlights and head-lights swept over the land. When his door opened, he didn't turn.

"Mom?"

"Tim, come on downstairs, okay? Those tapes came in the mail today. I thought we were going to watch a movie. I've already started the popcorn."

"Mom, are we gonna leave soon? You promised we would. I don't like it here anymore."

She stood behind him, hands on his shoulders. "Me, neither, twerp, but we have to hold on. Just a little while longer."

"When?"

Her arms draped over his shoulders and held him close. "Soon, honey, I promise. Soon."

He didn't like the answer.

It sounded like she was praying.

Wayman stood beside Marlin Bliss' truck, blowing on his gloved hands, stamping his feet to keep them

from going numb. The cashmere coat was classy, but
it didn't do diddly against this damn cold. "Jesus H.
Christ," he said angrily. "Are you telling me nobody
thought to stay back there with them?"

Bliss, his hat pulled low, rolled his eyes. "Well,
excuse me, Ike, but we had a little problem here,
remember?" He looked over the bed into the field
beyond. He could hear shouts and warnings and had
half a mind to fire the signal shot that would bring
them all back. If he did it now, they'd probably make
him a saint. "They ain't gonna find anything, Ike,
you now that. It's gonna be just like Kira and the
others."

Wayman's chest puffed as if he were going to blow
his stack and yell; instead, he sagged against the rear
fender and waved an apologetic hand. "I know, Mar,
I know. Sweet Jesus, don't I know."

Bliss folded his arms on the bed wall and shook
his head. "I hope Leb don't screw up. Somebody else
goes, you and I are gonna be the only ones left."

"That," said Wayman tightly, "is why I wanted
someone to stay back. I think our boy is getting ready
to run."

"So? Good riddance to bad rubbish, and the more
for the rest of us. He ain't the only one who can tell
a story."

"No," Wayman agreed, "but he's the only one who
can tell it right."

Vivian wondered what Proctor would say if he
knew how hard she had fought to be relieved of this

assignment even before it had begun. Her arguments had been basic: Proctor, by all accounts, could take care of himself; his personal cases were bizarre, to say the least, and Blaine was undoubtedly wasting his money; and just because Blaine didn't go to the office every day didn't mean he still didn't need watching over. There were too many enemies out there, in too many directions.

Blaine had listened attentively as he always did, and when she was finished, he only said, "Miss Chambers, I want my daughter back."

Period.

End of discussion.

Now, as she walked with Proctor toward the stables, aware that "the night has eyes" was much more than a cliché out here in the middle of nowhere, she hadn't changed her mind, but had to admit that this was . . . not exciting exactly, maybe intriguing. It was, if you looked at it one way, a whole lot better than sitting in New Jersey watching people work computers on a case that should have been filed ten years ago. Those women—

She stopped.

"Proctor."

He looked over his shoulder, stopped and faced her. "What?"

"Those women. Morning Star. Where are they? We've made enough noise to raise the dead. Where'd they go?"

He wiped a hand over his mouth and shrugged. "I don't know. I've been thinking the same thing myself." Then he waggled his eyebrows, looked pointedly at the stars and flapped his arms before moving on.

Oh, very funny, she thought; very funny.

But it took everything she had not to look up, too. Not because she thought he believed it, but because she had a bad feeling he didn't automatically discount the possibility. More things in heaven and earth, he had said, and in a place like this it was too easy to understand:

A Wild West town no bigger than a postage stamp, with no inhabitants she could find; the brush of their shoes across the ground; the sound of their breathing; the grassland out there beyond the reach of the light that made soft husking sounds even though there was no wind; the pale steam of her breath curling back to brush her cheeks like the touch of a—

Damnit!

She did look at the stars then, and cursed herself for it.

She hurried to catch up without seeming to hurry, hooked his shoulder with one hand and said, "What does this have to do with that con you mentioned before?"

"Later," he told her, keeping his voice low. "Leb should tell us most of what we need to know."

She didn't release him; she stopped and forced him to turn. "No more games," she told him. "I'm sick of your games."

Slowly he turned his head to look at her hand, slowly turned his head back to look at her. He didn't touch her, but she lowered her arm anyway, making it clear by how slowly she did it that there was no apology involved.

He said, voice low and even, "I don't play games."

She nodded. Once.

They walked together to the stable, its doors slightly ajar, and she reminded herself that it was cold out here, and that was why she felt the chill.

On the tracks just beyond the reach of the light, three figures in dark robes.

As they watched the man and woman approach the stable doors, the tallest one said, "I'm not sure about this."

"Patience," said Robin. "You told us we needed patience."

"Someone was not terribly patient about Otis Dugan."

The others didn't answer.

The air began to stir, lifting dust from the streets, spinning motes into the light.

"If we're wrong," the tall one said.

"Patience," Tie reminded her uncharacteristically uneasy leader. "You're not wrong."

Reluctantly the tall one nodded. "Fetch the others. Now. I'll meet you back at the ranch."

Neither Tie nor Robin turned as the tall one walked away, nor did they move when they heard the purr of a car's engine. But when it faded, Tie shook her head.

"It's a mistake," she said. "We can't let this go without doing something."

"Of course not," said Robin. "Besides, why should Ariel and Lark have all the fun?"

Tie laughed. "You're terrible."

And Robin answered, "Not yet."

THIRTEEN

Proctor reached for the stable door, hesitated, and called softly, "Leb? Leb Coster?"

A whimper inside, and he opened the door wider, let it swing of its own weight until it thumped softly against the wall and rebounded a few inches. He stepped in and paused, letting his vision adjust to the dim light, smelling the straw, the hay, the manure, the sweat. The unmistakable tang of alcohol.

And fear, as palpable as anything else.

When he heard the sound again, harsher, he looked down and saw Coster sitting against the wall, knees drawn tightly to his chest.

"You okay?"

Coster looked up, red-eyed and blinking. "What the hell do you think?" He wiped his nose with a sleeve, shuddered a deep breath. He didn't seem at all embarrassed that he'd been caught crying; he didn't seem to care one way or the other, not even when Vivian stepped inside, looked around, looked at him. But his gaze followed Proctor warily when he moved across the uneven floor and leaned back against a stall door.

"What do you want?"

"I've got some questions, Leb," Proctor said, hunching his shoulders briefly against the cold.

"No shit," the man grumbled. To Vivian: "Close the door, turn on the light, you brought up in a barn or something? Jesus Christ."

She found the light switch, flicked it up, and pulled on a length of rope attached to a rusted butterfly cleat on one of the doors until both were closed. Several small bulbs worked feebly in the high rafters. It wasn't much, but at least they could see. Then she leaned over him, put a hand on his shoulder, and squeezed.

"Next time," she said sweetly, "say please, okay?"

"Jesus!" Coster wrenched the shoulder away and rubbed it gingerly. Then, softer, "Damn," and stared at the floor, head hanging.

Proctor waited patiently, listening to a horse shift in its stall at the other end of the stable. As far as he could tell, it was the only animal in here. He didn't say anything about the half-empty bottle he saw at the man's side.

Coster dusted the already gleaming metal tips of his boots, brushed at his jeans, picked up a piece of straw from the floor and tossed it aside.

"Whenever you're ready," Proctor said evenly. "I'm in no hurry."

"Well you damn well better be," Coster snapped.

Swallowed. Shook his head miserably and blew out a long breath. "You're not a cop, right?"

Proctor shook his head.

"You got an open mind?"

"Maybe. Depends on what it's supposed to be open to."

"What about her?"

"Her," Proctor said flatly, "is standing right next to you. Why don't you ask?"

Coster scowled up at Vivian, whose smile made him turn immediately away. "You're gonna think I'm crazy."

"I don't think so."

"Okay." He rolled his shoulders, put his head back, and rubbed hard at his scalp. "Okay. But don't say I didn't warn you."

It started, the little man said, about three, four years ago, not long after we found out Morning Star was going to take over the Coglin ranch.

For a long time, the Junction had been struggling just to make ends meet. Years before, a decade or so after the TV and movie boom had ended, most of the farms around here had been gobbled up by larger operations that took their business elsewhere—closer to Wichita, Topeka, places like that. When the grain elevators burned to the ground during a lightning storm and the railroad stopped running, most people figured, hell it couldn't get much worse.

It did.

Around then, we still had a bunch of people commuting to the county seat, sometimes farther, bringing back regular paychecks, but there wasn't enough tourist or pass-through business to keep the town going on its own. Still, most everyone loved the Junction. Crime was pretty much nonexistent except when a drunk got to feeling his oats, the air was clean, the food homegrown, neighbors looked after neighbors . . . all in all, you couldn't ask for a better place to live.

Even the Morning Star people weren't all that big a problem. Sure, they tried to get people to join up once in a while, but in such a way that almost no one took offense. Even when, once in a great while, someone trooped off to the ranch, looking for inner peace, whatever the hell that was, nobody fussed except maybe family.

Besides, once those women got their operation going, they gave away practically everything they grew—vegetables and such; they spent money in town like it was going out of style; and they made a habit of helping folks out now and then, doing housecleaning and minor repairs, contributing all the tools and materials themselves. Without cost or, so they claimed, obligation.

It didn't take long before folks stopped talking about them, or making cracks that they were all women, or pointing out that no one ever saw them except after sundown. Vampire stories got a pretty good run there for a while, especially around Halloween.

I guess we got used to them.

Big mistake.

Late one summer, a young guy, a local stargazer, pitched a tent about a mile south of here, telling everybody he wanted to see some fool comet or other, pestering everyone to come out and join him. No one did; we thought he was kind of nuts. Late the next day one of his buddies got worried when he didn't come back and went out there to fetch him home.

He didn't find anything but a torn-up tent and his buddy's telescope and enough blood to fill a lake.

People blamed everything from a lost cougar out of Colorado to one of those homicidal maniacs to about forty dozen different monsters. Not that it made a difference, because neither the killer nor the boy's body were ever found.

The following spring it happened again. A woman walking along the tracks with her boyfriend after midnight. The boyfriend, just before they hauled him off to the nuthouse, kept saying it was something in the sky that had swooped down and attacked them. Nobody really believed him; they figured his own wounds, which were pretty awful themselves, had been the result of his lady friend fighting him off with the knife she'd been carrying.

Never found her body, though, and no explanations, official or otherwise, had ever been offered.

Just one of those mysteries like you see on the TV.

Then folks began hearing things late at night, walking home from wherever, standing on the porch, lying in bed with the windows open.

Something flying up there.

Something big.

Marlin Bliss' dog, a mean old German shepherd, he got out one night, Bliss chased him all over creation. He heard those sounds, those wing sounds. He heard his dog barking, then growling, then screaming. He . . . found the spot, but there was nothing left but blood and tufts of fur.

You saw Kenny, right?

His wife had run off to Morning Star a while back, sometime in June, I think it was. Last week sometime, she calls him, all scared and wanting to come home. Tells him they don't want her to go, but she's leaving anyway. Kenny, he's all pissed off because she left him in the first place, so he don't give a damn. Stay or come, he don't care. So Kira calls him one afternoon, says she's leaving that night after everyone goes to bed. It's a message on his answering machine, but he don't play it until late because he's too busy drinking. He drank just enough that she got him all pissed off again. Passed out. Next morning she's not back, he's feeling guilty, he gets in the car and heads for the ranch.

Less than a mile from the tracks he found some blood, a long piece of a shirt he'd given her for Christmas, some kind of velvet or something, and a beat-up flashlight.

Ike's on his way back from the county seat and finds Kenny sitting in the middle of the road, trying to mop up the blood with his shirt.

Maybe you saw them, Proctor.

I'm willing to bet you heard them.

They sound like wings, don't they.

They sound like . . . wings.

The mare in the far stall stamped the floor lightly.

The wind found hollow places in the eaves to give it a low voice.

One of the rafter bulbs was loose, and it flickered; shadows faded and jumped.

Proctor glanced at Vivian, who clearly didn't believe a word. But when she raised an eyebrow at him, all he did was raise one back and push the hair away from his forehead. He ignored Coster, who watched him expectantly, one eye partially closed, looking as if he were holding his breath. Proctor fussed with his hair again, turned and leaned into the empty stall. Nothing there but darkness. When he turned around, Coster's expression had turned to an angry frown.

"Good story."

Coster glared. "Good . . ." He struggled awkwardly to his feet, using the wall for balance, kicking the bottle over. The air filled with the stench of spilled liquor. "You goddamn son of a bitch, that thing killed Otis tonight, or hadn't you noticed?"

"I wouldn't know," he answered mildly. "I haven't seen any body, just a lot of people running around."

Trembling with anger, Coster pointed at the far stall. "That poor critter was covered with blood, damnit. You saw that, you son of a bitch, I know you did, I saw you looking. And it wasn't hers, I can tell you that for sure. You don't believe it, go look for yourself, the rags are over there in the corner, and she ain't got but a couple of scratches." His fists rose to the center of his chest and he stared at them as the knuckles whitened. "Kenny—"

"I know. We talked to him."

"Mr. Coster," Vivian said, matching Proctor's tone, "why did you tell us this? I mean, what's the point?"

Coster turned on her, face dangerously flushed, but when she shifted her weight from one foot to the other, he stepped back hurriedly, mouth working without a sound.

"Where's Leona Elmdorf?" Proctor asked.

Coster whirled to face him, suddenly confused. "What?"

"We followed your directions, Leb, but she wasn't home. The fact is, I'm under the impression she hasn't been home for quite a while." He stepped closer, and Coster backed into the wall. When Proctor reached into an inside pocket, the little man almost cringed, then blinked rapidly in bewilderment when Proctor held out the letter. "Who wrote this, Leb?" A soft voice. "Not you, I'd guess." A quick smile. "But I bet you know what it says." Another step, not stopping until there was only a handbreadth between them.

A sudden gust pushed against the doors, and dust drifted to the floor.

"Who wrote it, Leb?" Softer, and harder, his head turned almost sideways. "Is she one of the victims you haven't told me about, Leb, or did she leave on her own?" He tapped the letter against Coster's chest

lightly, and the little man flinched. A whisper now:
"Did this . . . thing . . . really do all the killing . . .
or was it one of you?"

"Jesus," Coster gasped. "I . . . Jesus!"

Although Proctor wasn't blocking him, the man
acted as if he couldn't move, as if he were trapped.
He looked to Vivian for help, but she only spread
her hands to say *hey, don't look at me, I'm not in charge
here, he is.*

The loose bulb flickered, and went out.

The mare stamped and snorted.

Another gust, and Coster stared at the door, licking
his lips, wiping his mouth.

Proctor stepped away and slipped his hands into
his coat pockets. A whisper: "Come on, Leb. You all
wanted to get me here, so I'm here, and I'd like to
know why. What, exactly, am I supposed to do?"

Vivian moved back, just far enough to slip her out
of the light, only a pale blur where her face should
have been.

Coster slumped against the wall, hooked a thumb
into his belt. His voice was so low, Proctor had to
concentrate to hear him: "Kill it."

Proctor nodded. "I see."

"Nobody believes us," Leb said quietly, bitterly.
"County doesn't care, they think we're all nuts. After
they got done not solving the first one, they figured
we were making the others up. To get attention. Get
someone over from Topeka to remember we're still
alive out here. Some kind of scheme, they said, and
sent Ike packing with his tail between his legs." He

looked up, mouth twisted. "People are disappearing here, and we're doing it to get attention for some measly state aid? I . . ." He shook his head, wiped his face.

"So somebody," Proctor said, "says they know somebody who knows somebody who's heard of me. Somebody else volunteers to write the letter, figuring they knew what it would take to get me out here."

Leb nodded miserably. "Yeah. That's about it."

The mare snorted, and kicked the wall lightly.

"Leona?"

Leb shrugged wearily; he had nothing left to lose. "She and her sister moved out five, six years ago. Some damn retirement place in Tampa, I think. We kept the place up in case somebody wanted to buy it." He barked a laugh. "Fat chance, huh?"

When the wind hit the door again, Proctor glanced at it and looked away. "So tonight was part of the con?"

"Hell, no! We was . . . shit, we was gonna—god-*damn*!" He hustled down the aisle when the mare kicked her stall again, hard and fast, sounding as if she were trying to break out. "Damnit, you goddamn idiot, calm down," he yelled. "You're gonna break your goddamn legs."

Then he yelped when the horse reached over the door, ears back, teeth bared, aiming for whatever part of him she could reach.

"Jesus, Proctor, can you give me a hand here?"

Proctor was about to tell him he didn't know the first thing about horses, when Vivian jumped back

from the wall at another gust and reached out to slap
a warning at his arm.

He didn't have to ask.

Whatever was out there, it wasn't the wind.

FOURTEEN

It hit the double doors high and hard, rattling them on their hinges, bouncing them open a crack until Vivian grabbed the rope and wrapped it quickly around the butterfly cleats. She jumped back as they shook again, thunder loud.

The mare grew frantic, and Coster bellowed at Proctor to for God's sake do something.

"What is it?" Vivian whispered.

Proctor drew his gun, watching the doors as he made sure the clip was in and the safety off.

Something hit the doors, lower, but not as hard.

He almost fired, and when Vivian gave him a look that demanded to know why he hadn't, he whispered back, "Maybe it's one of Leb's friends, back from the chase."

He didn't want to take a chance that this wasn't part of the con; he didn't want someone hurt, or worse, because he'd jumped without looking.

He motioned her over to stand at his left hand, ready to head toward the back in case anything went wrong.

Grit from the doors pattered softly onto the floor-boards, and a slow-swirling cloud of dust hung under the rafters.

The mare's initial panic had eased, but he could hear her still thumping, could hear Leb's desperate whispers—"Easy, girl, easy"—as he tried to keep her calm.

A look to Vivian and a shake of his head, and Proctor took a cautious step toward the doors, watching the faint light in the slender crack between them, the gap under them, head cocked, listening.

He didn't hear it, but he knew it—something was out there.

A faint scratching on the wood. Testing, not digging.

If it was human, the guy knew what he was doing. Catch them in a mostly dark and unfamiliar place, push all the buttons. Loud noises, soft noises, periods of dead silence. Let those inside trigger their imaginations and let that do the work for him.

Make them believe there really was a creature out there.

On the other hand, Leb was right. He had heard the wings.

The glow beneath the doors flickered as something passed, and returned.

Scratching, faint and steady.

All right, he thought; all right, in for a penny.

He leaned close to Vivian and whispered, "Tell Leb to brace himself, I'm going to take a shot."

She opened her mouth to protest, nodded sharply

and hurried away, so silently he had to look to be sure she had gone. Then he tried to pinpoint the site of the noise—scratching, lightly scratching—and figured it was just about head high. A check over his shoulder, Vivian waved an okay, and he aimed at the upper frame.

He fired.

The gunshot was cannon-loud, the muzzle flash lightning-bright; chips and splinters of old wood made him duck, swearing at himself when he heard the poor mare buck and cry, heard Leb curse obscenely.

Good move, he told himself sourly, and moved closer to the doors. Listening. Watching the bars of light, which were unblocked now and filled with floating dust.

His left hand rose, a hopeful signal of victory, until he heard it again—the scratching on the wood. Still testing. A little harder.

Damn; and he aimed again, this time at the spot where he thought the outsiders might be. Too bad, now, if they were human; they had pushed him just a little too far.

The doors began to shake.

Slowly at first, as someone pushed against them, testing the strength of the rope's makeshift lock. Reluctantly he lowered the gun as more than one body blocked the glow beneath, and the doors shook more vigorously, the rope around the cleats beginning to unwind. He reached out to grab it, wind it tighter, and jumped back with a startled oath when a heavy object slammed against the middle.

It wouldn't take long; the rope was old and fraying.

He fired once and turned and ran, skidding to a halt at the last stall. Leb was on the adjoining wall, straddling it as he talked to the mare, reaching out to stroke it and snapping his hand back whenever the horse turned her teeth toward him.

"Another way out?"

Leb pointed at a door Proctor hadn't seen before in the sidewall. "Goes through the tack room into the store."

"We can't stay."

The double doors bowed under a violent sustained shaking, shuddering when they were struck again in the center.

"She'll kill herself," Leb said plaintively, reaching for the old horse. Then, angrily, "Goddamnit, can't you do something?"

A lightbulb flared and popped out directly overhead.

"Do you have something?" Vivian asked him. "Protection?"

The mare tossed her head, flinging foam and spittle.

Leb pointed to the corner, and Proctor saw a rifle propped in the corner.

"Use it," she ordered, opened the door, looked back once, and went through.

A large crack opened in one of the doors, spilling in light and clouds of dust.

"Do what she says," Proctor told him, and made to follow, paused on the threshold when Coster snapped his name.

"Do you believe me now?"

He didn't answer. At the same time Vivian called him to hurry, he saw the mare, white-eyed and thrashing, collapse to the floor. Leb wailed and jumped in after her. Proctor hesitated until Vivian called him again, and he ran through the narrow tack room into the shop beyond, following her to the front where she stopped, breathing heavily.

"Flank them," she said jerking her head toward the corner only a few yards away. "If we don't get them, maybe we can chase them away." She reached low into her jacket and pulled out a gun with a barrel so long it made his eyes widen. She grinned and yanked open the door. "Tell you about it sometime. I have a name for it, but it's disgusting."

Main Street was deserted.

The wind had died; nothing moved, and no one was visible in any of the shop windows.

After a quick check, Vivian jumped lightly to the street; he stayed on the sidewalk. Together they sprinted to the end of the building, and at a brusque nod from him, leapt around the corner and crouched, guns out and ready.

Nothing was there.

He hadn't realized until now how far apart the

hooded bulbs were, high on the wall, and didn't like the spotlight effects they created. At the same time, he wished someone had used higher wattage; they barely made a downward scoop on the building, and didn't do well illuminating the blacktop, much less the five-foot-wide border of dirt that separated the blacktop from the stable walls.

It was like slipping into fog.

Without waiting for the questions, he eased forward, one slow step at a time, keeping his right shoulder close to the building. Fighting the unnerving feeling there was a target on his spine. Squinting ahead into the dark that lay beyond the light's reach, once in a while catching a glint of mica or broken glass in the weeds that choked the track embankment, while Vivian concentrated on the roof and the sky.

He had no intention of moving beyond the doors, into the area where there was no light at all. He signaled to her, received a *good move* nod in return as she angled closer to the far edge of the blacktop while keeping abreast, watching his back, moving with such grace that he had to stop himself from staring.

One step at a time.

Swallowing dryly, forcing himself to blink when he found himself staring too long, hearing only his own breathing and the slide of his soles over the hard-packed earth.

Ten feet from the doors he began to search the ground and the incline that led up to the stable entrance, saw disturbances in the dirt and dirt kicked onto the street. He moved away from the building, scanning the doors and wall as best he could at the distance, trusting Vivian to watch the rest, and him.

He stopped when he reached the foot of the incline, frowned, and finally lowered the gun.

Well, he thought.

Vivian came up beside him, standing sideways, tense, almost bouncing. "Are we going to chase them?"

He looked around pointedly. "Where?"

"Right." She checked the ground around their feet. "I don't see any rocks or timber."

"Nope."

"So what did they use, a battering ram?"

"I don't know."

Portions of the doors, at the top and in the center, had mild indentations, hardly the kind of damage to wood that a body could do. The best result would have been a broken or dislocated shoulder. He rubbed his own shoulder absently, imagining the force. Moving closer, he was unable to find scores or gouges where the scratching had been, and the ground was too hard to hold footprints.

And as long as he was at it, he wondered why whoever it was tried to batter the doors inward. They opened out. Anyone in town would know that, and he supposed the Morning Star women would know it, too. It would have been easier, in degree, to yank, not pound.

He squatted, hands draped over his knees as he

examined the dirt at the base of the doors, not staring but letting his gaze roam, turning slightly right on the balls of his feet, then left. Small stones, hard earth, until he spotted something.

He rose slowly, wincing when one of his knees popped.

His weapon went back into its holster, and he zipped his jacket up. Flexed his fingers and wished he'd thought to bring gloves. With his left arm out to keep Vivian back he walked across the incline and crouched again by the left-hand door's bottom hinge.

Here, the incline sloped gently a good six feet toward the rear of the building. Unlike the area that led into the stable, it was ridged by years of running water, and hot summers, frigid winters. A large sharp-edged rock had been partially exposed by the erosion, with something caught on its near face.

"What?" Vivian asked quietly.

He picked it up with two fingers and held it so she could see.

At first she didn't recognize it, but when he stood and lay it out across her palm, her eyes widened in surprise. She looked at the doors, at his hand, at the doors again, and said, "Can't be. I mean . . . it can't be."

"Sure it can," he said.

In his hand lay several tangled strands ripped or torn from the tassel of a monk's robe girdle.

FIFTEEN

Proctor stood on the blacktop at the bottom of the incline, his back to the stable, hands in his pockets. At his insistence, Vivian left to check on Leb and the mare. She hadn't wanted to leave him, but he assured her the incident was over for now. They were alone, and to her credit she didn't ask how he knew.

That, he wouldn't have been able to tell her.

He just knew.

Just as he knew that this elaborate con game couldn't have been set up solely by the people who lived in this town. He'd had no time to think it through, it was only what Taz would call a deep gut feeling, but once planted he couldn't shake the suspicion that an outsider was involved.

He pursed his lips in a silent whistle.

You believe that? he asked himself; you really believe that?

Later, he answered, and grinned as if Vivian were standing beside him; think about it later.

Right now . . .

He lifted his face toward the sky, breathing deeply. The night air, despite its cold, was refreshing after the closeness of the stable. No scent of fear. No lingering harsh scents of the animals who used to live in those stalls.

Breathing deeply; letting his nerves calm, the adrenaline settle.

He considered getting angry at the scheme that had brought him here; he considered fetching Vivian and the car, and heading back into Colorado, to the ranch and the airstrip where the plane waited to take him home. But the former would be a waste of time and probably make him do something stupid, and the latter would inevitably turn into a lasting regret.

The curse of needing to know all the answers.

Here under the light, however dim, most of the stars were washed-out; he couldn't see the moon at all. Still, he looked up and wondered how they did it, the wing sounds, the stable assault which, when hindsight considered it, wasn't much of an assault at all; the scratching that had left no marks that he could see.

Pushing buttons, that's all; just pushing a few buttons.

All part of a con that, he admitted with less than a shade of grace, had worked.

Turning around by stages he peered at the overhanging eaves on the high roofline, then directed his gaze up and across Main Street. Speakers up there, maybe. Given the darkness and the silence, and the mood he'd been in, they would have done the job; simple and cheap.

But if that was true, the con didn't make sense. If that was true, there had to be something Coster hadn't told him. He rubbed an earlobe lightly. Did they want him to get rid of Morning Star? That made even less sense. By the little man's own account, the women had actually done the town some good. A lot of good, in fact.

His fingers passed over the strands of the tassel in his pocket, and he glanced once more at the battered stable doors.

A lot of good; no price, no obligation.

Yes, there was, he thought; one way or another there's always a price, there's always an obligation.

He blew out a swift loud breath and headed toward the corner. Coster had a few more questions coming, and if he didn't give the answers Proctor wanted, there was always one of the others.

When they returned, that is.

He started, then, when Vivian suddenly appeared at the corner.

"Leb," she said.

"What about him?"

"That horse is dead, and he's gone."

Proctor took the corner at a slow trot, staying in the street, heading for the Gold Star until, halfway there, he changed his mind. Hazel had told him the Gold Star was for eaters, the Diamond Sal for drunks; if Coster hadn't beat it to his friends, or run home to hide, he probably figured a bottle was about as good a friend as he had right now.

He headed up to the second saloon, not really hurrying, slowing to a brisk walk. If he was right, Coster wasn't going anywhere; if he was wrong, it was Coster's territory, not his.

Vivian remained on the sidewalk, keeping pace, her long-barrel vanished back into her coat. "It was awful," she said as he veered closer.

He nodded; he could imagine.

At the intersection they both glanced left and right, checking for shadows that shouldn't be there. As satisfied as he could be under the circumstances that they were alone, he climbed to the sidewalk and paused in front of the entrance, which was angled to face the corner. The batwing doors he had noted their first time through were actually painted on glass, better protection against the cold and coming winter. From a distance they had looked real.

But then, so did Hart Junction.

"I found the rags," she told him. "The bloody rags, the ones he used to clean her off. And a bucket with bloody water." She rubbed her hands together. "She was old, Proctor. I don't know much about horses, but you could tell she was old."

He nodded, looked up the street at the Gold Star, and said, "They're taking a hell of a long time out there."

"It's a hell of a big place out there, in case you hadn't noticed."

He grunted and went inside, letting Vivian catch the door on the backswing.

The interior was a mirror image of the Gold Star; the only exceptions were a half dozen square posts that supported the low ceiling, sawdust dusted here and there across the floorboards, and a brass footrail on the bar, with high and matching curve-back stools. He doubted the bottles lined up in front of the mirror were filled with colored water.

The chandeliers were unlit; what illumination there was came from electric candles on the walls and ceiling posts, and not all of them were working.

The only person in the room was Leb Coster.

He didn't look up as they approached him. He poured himself half a glass from an unlabeled bottle, toasted his reflection mockingly and took a long drink. When he came up for air, he grinned and waved. "Hey, you guys found me, you didn't die." He gestured to either side. "Grab a stool, set a while, when I fall off, you can carry me home."

Vivian stopped at the end of the bar, propping her elbows on the polished top, hooking a heel over the rail. After pushing her sleeves up, she folded her hands under her chin. Her expression was carefully blank.

Proctor moved to Coster's right, so he could lean against the bar and watch him and Vivian at the same time.

Coster shoved the bottle over. "Bourbon," he said, his words already slurred. "Hurts like hell going down, but I don't give a shit." He grinned stupidly. "Hell, it's free, right?"

Proctor said nothing.

A sharp *damn right* nod, and Leb's head began to sink as if it were too heavy for his neck to support. He sighed, wiped his mouth with the back of his hand, and drank again. "Stupid son of a bitch." He stared at the mirror, at Proctor's reflection. "You tell me . . . you tell me what a damn old man was doing the hell out there after sundown, huh? You tell me that."

"I don't know," Proctor said, pushing the bottle back.

"He knew better, you know." Coster refilled his glass, concentrating intently on not spilling the raw-smelling liquor. "He knew better. God damn idiot." His face was pale, red-rimmed eyes grotesque against the pallor. "Damn shithead idiot. Hasn't got the brains God gave a clam."

A draft coiled through the saloon, slipped around Proctor's ankles.

Coster straightened abruptly, stretched his neck, then leaned over the bar, fumbled behind it for a moment, and brought up another bottle. "Zona's not here," he said to Vivian as if she had disapproved. "You see him? Zona? Before, in the street? Goddamn bigass guy, hair down to his ass practically, black as night, I swear he gets it out of a bottle, you know what I mean? You see him?"

Vivian shrugged one shoulder. "I might have, I don't remember."

"Oh, you'd remember, all right. Bigass son of a bitch. Thinks he's a goddamn movie star." He snorted, smacked his lips, snorted again. "Zona Temple. 'Course that ain't his real name, you know. He just thinks it sounds good. Short for Arizona. Some kind of cowboy, the stupid son of a bitch thinks. Hell, he's only a bartender. What the hell kind of name is that for a bartender?"

Proctor watched his cheeks sink, watched his lips grow taut to stop their trembling.

"She's dead," Coster said quietly, hands wrapped around his glass.

Proctor said, "I know," just as quietly.

"Scared to death, you know that, right?" He shook his head sadly. "Poor old thing never did anything to nobody, that fatheaded Otis takes her out where he ain't supposed to be . . . couldn't take it when it came to get us back in there. Poor old thing couldn't take it anymore."

"Leb—"

"Otis, he treated her like a kid, you know? Pampered her like she was his kid." He swallowed hard. "Ah, shit. Ah, shit."

Proctor heard the wind, watched the sawdust stir.

Suddenly Coster laughed, slammed a palm on the bar and laughed again. "Jesus, Merle is gonna shit a brick, you know that? She is just gonna shit a brick!"

"Who's Merle?"

The little man looked at him as if he were stupid. "Well, Jesus, man, she's Otis' wife, ain't she? Married damn near forever, riding that mare was the only

thing she ever let him do on his own, the poor slob."
A shuddering laugh. "You know, she looks like Mrs.
Claus. You know that? You ever see her?"

"No, Leb, I never had the pleasure."

"Telling you straight, she looks like Mrs. Santa
Claus. Just like in the movies. Little old lady. Sweet
as all them cookies she makes for—" He froze. His
chin trembled. "Aw, shit, Proctor, who's gonna tell
Merle her old man is dead?" He shook his head pon-
derously. "Man, this'll kill her for sure."

He picked up the glass, but Proctor took his wrist,
holding it while Coster tried to figure out why he
couldn't take a drink.

When he did, his face reddened, his eyes narrowed, and he tried to slap the hand away.

"You know what she's gonna do?" he said, swallowing the sobs that began to rise in his throat, make
his breathing hitch. "She's gonna keep those damn
lights on until all the bulbs die, that's what she's
gonna do." He covered Proctor's hand with his, but
didn't try to pry it loose. "All those lights, it's gonna
drive the neighbors nuts." He smacked his lips
loudly. "Aw, shit."

Proctor watched him, encouraging him without a
word.

Coster's eyes closed briefly; when they opened
again, he shuddered. "Drives Otis nuts, you know.
Keeps 'em on even in the daytime. Claims it keeps
all the bad luck away." He smiled, and winked.
"Hasn't been right for a couple of years, if you know

what I mean. Jesus, Proctor, you gonna let me drink or what?"

Proctor removed his hand, and Coster emptied the glass in a singled long swallow. Coughed so hard he nearly toppled off the stool. Sobbed so hard he lowered his head to the bar and rocked back and forth, fingers still clutching the bottle.

"Leb."

Muffled: "Go away."

Proctor grabbed the man's shoulder and shook it. "Leb."

"Go the hell away!"

Proctor slid the bottle from his loose grip and batted the hand away when it tried to retrieve it. "Leb, where does Merle live?"

Coster reached. "Gimme the damn bottle!"

"You can have the whole bar for all I care. Just as soon as you tell me where this woman lives."

Coster blinked heavily, puffed his cheeks as he tried to think, then reached for the bottle again, cackling when Proctor let him have it. "That way," he said pointing at the back of the room. "Couple of blocks, three in from the corner." He cackled again. "Same as old Leona, the stupid old bitch. Hell, you go blind at night, staring at her damn house," and he laughed again as he tilted the bottle to his lips, not giving a damn that most of the liquor spilled through his beard onto his chest and lap. "Mrs. Claus." He belched, and laughed.

Vivian moved then. She lifted the bar's end flap and went behind, scanning the lower shelves. "Leb, when you get a storm, does Zona use candles or flashlights?"

Coster stared at her dumbly.

"Never mind." She disappeared for a moment, came up with two flashlights.

"You won't need 'em," Leb said. "I'm telling you, you won't need 'em." He stared at himself in the mirror. "Aw, shit, who's gonna tell her?"

Proctor headed for the door.

"You can't miss it," Coster called after him. "It's like Christmas over there. Tell her I said hi. Tell her that fool horse is dead."

Proctor didn't answer; he had already begun to run before he reached the exit.

SIXTEEN

Vivian tossed him one of the flashlights as they ran down the wide alley, and he fumbled it, nearly dropped it, and in the midst of the juggling act she took hold of the back of his coat and tugged to slow him down.

"No hurry," she said bluntly. "The lights were already out."

Yeah, he thought, and we were already there and maybe we could have done something.

He hadn't realized he'd spoken aloud until she said, "And maybe there's nothing we could have done because there's nothing wrong, Proctor." She came abreast as they crossed the street into the next alley. "Maybe she just turned out the lights."

She was right. Maybe. And that only made him angry, because this place was driving him nuts.

No, he thought; he was letting it drive him nuts.

They swung around the corner, and he pointed at the third house. The house lights they had noticed before were dark, and the corner streetlamp looked awfully far away.

He slowed to a walk.

There was no hedge or fence, just a slate walk to a house not much bigger than a bungalow. Vivian veered to the right and crossed the lawn, her light darting over low shrubs at the base of a small two-step porch barely wider than the front door. His own light, flickering bright and dim, swept over the front, bouncing back at him from the windows and from a single tiny pane in the front door.

He knocked; he rang the bell; he tried the doorknob and cursed when it wouldn't turn.

"Proctor," Vivian called, and he didn't like the sound of her voice.

As he made his way toward her, he checked the side windows, but the flashlight showed him nothing but drawn shades and fleeting patches here and there of peeling paint. She waited in the backyard, light pointed at the ground.

"What?"

The light moved and centered on a wooden stoop and a door that had been slammed open, its center wood crosspiece split and bowed, the frame exploded at the lock.

"Oh . . . hell," he muttered. A quick check of the yard first, the white beam passing over two trees, a rectangular patch of earth that had to be a garden, and an empty birdbath. Nothing else.

He didn't want to go in.

"Maybe," she said nervously, "we should wait for those guys to get back."

What for? he asked silently; it isn't going to change anything in there.

He was a step away from the door when he smelled it and said, "Damn," so forcefully Vivian stopped where she was. He said, "Listen."

The wind had calmed to a steady breeze that felt laced with ice.

"What?" she asked quietly. "I don't hear—"

When she stopped, he knew she'd heard it, too, and if she had any imagination at all, she knew what it meant.

It was the drone of feeding flies.

He aimed his light at the threshold, a ridged aluminum strip worn by age and use. Farther, and he saw a black-and-white-tiled floor; higher, to a square table with four captain's chairs around it.

"Oh, my God," Vivian said at his shoulder, her light merged with his.

The floor, the table, the counters and walls were white, and black, and spattered with gleaming blood.

"Don't," she warned as he went in.

"Too late."

Avoiding the blood as best he could, he made his way around the table toward a doorway on the other side. "Mrs. Dugan!" he yelled. "Mrs. Dugan, if you can hear me, say something, make a noise!"

Nothing but the flies, which barely stirred when he passed them.

"Proctor, come on," Vivian urged from the back door.

He checked the ceiling and found some dark spots

that told him nothing of what had happened. At the doorway he stopped, and nearly gagged.

"Proctor?"

"Stay there," he said hoarsely.

"Is it . . . bad?"

He didn't answer.

The small living room was where the attack happened—an armchair on its side and gutted, a couch shredded and its stuffing scattered over the carpet, a turned-over standing lamp, a step ladder on its side. Broken glass. Gouged and splintered wood. A lampshade's wire frame lying near the front door.

He didn't bother to look for something not touched by the blood.

"Proctor, what is it?"

"Butcher shop," was all he said.

He sank slowly to his heels, pressing his left hand against the jamb for balance, let the flashlight shift slowly over the floor, over the shimmering bodies of crawling bloated flies, until it stopped almost at his feet. He swallowed, reached out and picked up what he saw.

"What are you doing?" Vivian said. "This is a crime scene, Proctor, you know better than that."

It was a hair net, the kind favored by old women of a certain age and time, and in it was caught a large clump of filmy white.

Mrs. Claus.

He rose carefully, with no intention of going in there, no intention of searching the rest of the house. He stuffed the hair net into his pocket, opened his mouth to call again, and changed his mind, closed his eyes for a moment before turning around.

Water dripped from the kitchen faucet.

Behind him, blood dripped from something else.

He could feel his face change as he crossed the kitchen, could feel it harden and grow warm; he could feel his heartbeat, too steady, too calm, for what he'd just seen.

"That's not a crime scene," he said as he passed her on the stoop. "That's a slaughterhouse."

As he walked away from the house, exhaling sharply to drive the scent of blood from his nostrils, he felt sorry for Vivian, and not a little admiration. She hadn't asked to be involved with either Black Oak or him, clearly hadn't imagined being involved in something like this, yet still hadn't mounted her own insurrection.

Had she done so, he wouldn't have blamed her.

And suddenly surprised himself by realizing he didn't want her to.

The wind picked up, but he barely felt it, and ignored the way his hair crawled spiderlike across his brow.

"What now?" she asked as they fairly marched through the alley.

"The police."

"You think they'll believe us?"

"What's not to believe? We found a house where an obvious assault has taken place. Murder, most likely, it can't be anything else. In a town where apparently similar events have occurred over the past few years."

"But what about the . . . whatever you call it?"

He looked at her profile, faint and too pale. "I didn't see it. Did you?"

She didn't look back. "No. But to tell you the truth, I think I'm hearing footsteps."

"Better than wings," he said with almost a grin.

"In this town, what's the difference?"

Back on the main street there was no sign of Otis Dugan's search party. Dust hazed the lights, dimmed the stars.

She stopped him at the corner, tilted her head toward the Diamond Sal, and said, "What about him?"

"What about him?"

"Proctor, we can't . . ." She shook her head. "The house."

He didn't argue; there was no point and he wouldn't have won anyway. Once inside, however, he wished he'd said something.

Coster lay on the bar, snoring wetly, hands folded on his chest as if he'd been laid out for a wake. There was a shattered bottle on the floor, and the mirror was webbed where another one had struck it.

"Jesus," Proctor muttered, kicked two stools out of the way, and crouched so that Vivian could roll the unconscious man onto his shoulder, feet dangling down his back, head bumping against his stomach.

Coster moaned but didn't waken.

"If he throws up on my coat," Proctor said grimly as they hurried across the street, "you get to clean it."

"Not in this lifetime."

He didn't slow down or shift when he reached the Gold Star. Coster's head whacked open the batwing doors, and he moaned again.

"Serves you right," Proctor said, and dumped him onto the bar as he bellowed, "Hazel! Hazel, get in here!"

The kitchen door swung open hard enough to strike the wall, but when she came in, glaring and wiping her hands on her apron, he gave her no time to demand explanations. "I need a phone. The police."

"For what, him?" she said, sneering at Coster.

"Someone's killed Mrs. Dugan," he answered curtly. "Now where the hell is that phone?"

Mouth open, one hand fluttering toward her throat, she pointed vaguely at the kitchen, then reached behind her to find a chair. "My God." When she found it, she sat quickly. "My God."

"Vivian," Proctor said with a nod toward the kitchen, "would you?" He moved around the table and sat facing the bar and Hazel, who had pulled out a tissue and held it to her mouth. "Hazel, you have to talk to me."

Her eyes began to fill with tears, and she had a difficult time swallowing.

He kept his voice low. "Leb told me about what's going on, getting me out here, your troubles in the past." He took the letter from his pocket and placed it on the table beside her. She stared at it, blinked, caught a tear with the tissue before it reached her cheek. "Did you write this?" He put the flyer with it. "The note is yours, too?"

Another tear, but this one she let fall. She nodded.

He leaned forward. "Well, it worked, Hazel. I'm here, and I have no idea what the hell is going on."

"The wings," she said, voice quivering.

"I've heard them."

Vivian stood in the kitchen doorway. "The phone is dead."

Madness, Proctor thought; madness.

"Get Kenny to show you how the lights work. Turn them off back here, leave them on in front."

"Proctor—"

"Please, Vivian, do as I ask."

After she left, he rubbed his fingers across his forehead, couldn't help smelling blood on his sleeve even though it was clean. "This isn't part of it, is it," he said. "Otis and his wife, Leb said this isn't part of the plan."

Hazel covered her eyes, shook her head.

"So tell me what I'm dealing with here. Local legends? Indian burial grounds? Someone put a curse on the town? What are the wings, Hazel? What are they?"

She made such an effort to stop the tears that he feared she would faint—her jaw tightened, her eyes closed, her neck trembled, she held her breath for an unnervingly long time. When she finally exhaled, it was a long slow sigh.

The lights dimmed around the walls, and only the front chandelier remained lit. For anyone outside, it would be difficult to see someone sitting near the stage.

"Leb said it all started when Morning Star moved in."

Hazel stiffened as if pricked with a pin.

"Is it something of theirs? Something they keep at the ranch?"

When she stared at him, he saw the red in her eyes, the star-points of mascara where the tears had tried to smear it. He might not have noticed the flushed center of her cheeks had not the rest of her face been so pale.

He waited patiently.

Vivian returned to stand behind the bar, but he didn't look over, not even when Kenny joined her.

He concentrated on Hazel, for a disconcerting moment in the faint light seeing her there as she had been years ago—without the weight or the heavy makeup or the stark red hair. When it passed, he saw a smile on her lips that vanished as soon as he recognized it for what it was—her own recognition of what he'd been thinking.

"What is it?" he asked gently.

"You—" She cleared her throat harshly. "You want to know what I think? Or what they think?"

"Both."

She didn't answer right away. She stalled by moving her chair so that she faced the table squarely, hands on the top, loosely clasped with the tissue trapped inside; she stalled by clearing her throat again and studying her hands as she rubbed her thumbs together.

She stalled, and Proctor waited.

"There aren't many of us, you know," she finally said.

He allowed her a smile. "I know. Leb forgot to change his boots when he came back with the cane."

Over her shoulder he saw Vivian start, then stare suspiciously at Kenny, who hadn't said a word since he entered the room.

Hazel shook her head. "It was a dumb stunt."

"It almost worked. Except for the boots."

"Mr. Proctor, they think it's some kind of bird or something those women have. They think those women do the killings first, then let the bird, maybe there's more than one of them, do the awful stuff later."

"Why?"

"To scare us out."

"Why? Is the town sitting on oil or gold or uranium or something?"

"No."

"Then why?"

"I don't know." She looked up. "I swear to God I don't know. The houses get bought, like Bill's and Leona's. That's all I know. The houses get bought."

He didn't think she was lying, but she was definitely afraid to tell him the whole truth.

Whose idea? he wondered, and again the notion of an outsider nudged him, and vanished.

First things first.

"Okay. That's what *they* think. What do *you* think?"

"*She* thinks," said Robin from the front of the room, "that I can fly."

And she lifted her arms and flapped them as she laughed.

SEVENTEEN

In a small room of the main house at the Coglin ranch, the Morning Star leader sat on the edge of the bed and tried to remain calm enough to make a rational decision.

Obviously things were already threatening to fall apart.

The discipline which had been successfully forced upon the four women had weakened considerably, disastrously. Otis Dugan should not have died. Otis Dugan, like Bill Albright and the Elmdorf sisters, should have been taken care of the usual way—with money.

There was no sense to the man's death. None at all.

The leader had no compunctions about murder. It was, at times, the only viable alternative. As long, of course, as it did not draw unnecessary attention.

Perhaps it should have been foreseen that, having once drawn blood without consequence, the women should grow to like it. Enjoy it. Worse; not plan for it, but spill it on a whim.

Perhaps it had been a mistake to create Morning Star at all.

With discipline's collapse, it was certainly a mistake to get Proctor out here.

Proctor, unlike the others, would fight.

Proctor, unlike the others, would demand answers as he fought.

And Proctor, if all the accounts were accurate, would not settle for the answers the Junction had been primed to give him.

Three possibilities then: the first, and best, would be that Proctor dies in the fighting. End of Proctor, end of problem.

The second would be that Proctor succeeds long enough so that he uncovers the answers the leader did not want him to have. Even if he died at the end, he would make sure those answers would get back to those who could do something about them.

And if he lived . . .

The leader groaned aloud.

Then: "Stop it, damnit! Stop it!"

Proctor was not superhuman; he was definitely not immortal. If he lived, there would be other times, in other places, for him to get his due.

The primary concern, however, was the here and now.

All was not yet lost.

The leader smiled. To use a favorite phrase, should there be a failure there was always the soothing balm of damage control. And no one was better at soothing balm and damage control than the leader.

Patience, then.

Be optimistic.

The leader laughed.

Fine, be optimistic all you want, but in the meantime, maybe you ought to pack.

Just in case.

Marlin Bliss fired three quick shots into the air, turned to Wayman, and said, "Screw it, let's go home."

Wayman nodded absently as he watched flashlights jump and bob their way toward him. He hadn't believed they would ever find more than those few puddles of blood on the side of the road, but there was only that one chance, and it had to be taken.

His immediate concern was Leb. Unlike Bliss, he didn't trust the runt to do his job properly. Proctor might listen, but he doubted the man would believe without the others around for immediate corroboration and support. Leb was good, but sometimes sloppy.

Bliss hadn't talked to Proctor; Wayman had.

All trails had an end, one way or another, and if Leb blew it, even a little, and Proctor got to the end and found him there, Wayman didn't think even the Morning Star leader would be able to save Leb's hide.

"Marlin," he said, forcing lightness into his voice, "do you realize I came all the way out here and forgot my damn gun?"

Bliss chuckled. "No shit, Ike. I'm supposed to be surprised?"

"Do you have an extra I can borrow?"

"Why? It's over."

Wayman looked pointedly at the sky. "Maybe. Maybe not."

EIGHTEEN

Vivian watched the black woman giggle, covering her mouth with long fingers, like a child. Something about the sound made her angry, and chilled her. It was forced, not spontaneous, not natural. She was ready to reach for her gun, but a glance from Proctor stopped her.

"And you can't fly, I suppose," he said.

Hazel gasped behind hands pressed hard to her lips.

Robin giggled again, flapped her arms a second time, and shrugged elaborately as she stared downward to point out that her feet were still connected to the floor. When she looked up, her hands were back in her sleeves, and a smile bared her teeth and upper gums.

Checking us out, Vivian thought; seeing who's here and who's not. Mocking. She's mocking us.

She didn't know what to do until she heard a faint whimper behind her, looked and saw Kenny sitting on the floor. Hiding. Curled tightly, his hands covering his head.

He believes it too: the flying.

She had half a mind to wake Coster up and let him see who had joined them.

"So what do you want?" Proctor asked mildly.

Robin headed for the street. "Peace," she said over her shoulder. "Understanding. What else is there?"

The doors swung shut behind her, she turned left, and was out of sight. When she didn't pass the long front window, Vivian moved.

"No," Proctor said.

She ignored him; she had had enough.

She walked steadily to the end of the bar, lifted the flap and passed through, letting it slam down behind her. The hasty scrape of a chair told her Proctor was moving as well, but she didn't look back. She slapped through the doors, ready for bear, and stopped.

Left; she was positive the woman had turned left.

There was no one in the street.

Eyes narrowed, she stepped off the sidewalk and slowly backed away from the building, checking the second-floor porch, shaking her head when she realized Robin would have to be lightning fast to be up there already. And disappear, because there were only two tall windows facing the street, both of them closed, their curtains unmoving. The spindles beneath the waist-high railing were too far apart to offer any cover, and unlike the porch on the other saloon, this one didn't wrap around.

Hands tapping her sides, she looked west, looked east, absolutely refused to look up.

She had a sudden thought as Proctor left the building, and dropped to her hands and knees to peer under the sidewalk. It was too dark, and she crawled over, refusing to explain. The man knew so damn much, he could figure it out himself.

But all he said was, "Use the flashlight," and she jerked it out of her pocket, muttered at the fact that it had begun to fade, and saw nothing under there but dirt, scraps of paper, low mounds of things she didn't want to know about.

When she gave up and rocked back onto her heels, Proctor was beside her, hands in his pockets.

"I figure about twenty, twenty-five of them counting the kid," he said, squinting when a gust signaled the wind had returned, stronger now, and colder. "They left in pairs and bunches, came back a few minutes later in different clothes, just different enough—makeup and false noses, maybe, wigs, I don't know—so we wouldn't catch on. We weren't looking at them all that hard, they stayed at the back, so it was easy to miss."

"Except for the boots," she said sarcastically.

"Yep. Except for the boots."

"Why the hell would they want to go through all that trouble?"

"One of our mysteries, Vivian. Just one of our mysteries. Like the dead telephone. The dead woman."

She grunted. "Actors. It's all been acting, right?"

"Looks like it. You want something else to think about?"

"No."

"If they're *all* acting, who's directing?"

She put the heel of one hand to her forehead, pressed, rubbed, and shoved the hand back through her hair. A glance at her watch and she almost groaned aloud. They hadn't been here but three hours, and already it felt as if she'd been here a lifetime.

Proctor blew on his hands to warm them. "I also figure Mrs. Dugan knew her killer."

She rose, ignoring the offer of his outstretched hand. She had reached the same conclusion when she had seen that the front door hadn't been damaged, realized that the back door had been busted open from the inside. What she didn't understand was why the killer hadn't just opened it. Unless he had panicked. Or was out of his mind with whatever rage drove him.

Or . . .

She closed her eyes tightly: no, don't even think about thinking that.

"Hey," he said.

"Hey what."

"I don't think I want to wait until morning before taking a look at Morning Star."

She stared at him incredulously. "You want to go out there now?"

His voice matched the shadows that flocked in the street. "You may have noticed it's panic time around here. Things are going wrong."

"So what? They've tricked you, Proctor. They—"

"People are dead."

She opened her mouth, closed it, tapped a foot in frustration. "You don't really owe them, you know."

"I'm not doing it for them. Not now."

She turned away from the look on his face. "So why pick on Morning Star? Why not . . . I don't know why not the banker and his buddies?"

He pulled the strands from his pocket. "Did you take a good look at Robin's tassel? It was looking a little ragged to me."

"You're kidding." She turned toward the stable, looked back at him. "Why didn't you call her on it?"

He replaced the strands. "Those people in there, Hazel and Kenny, they're more than scared, they're terrified. I don't know if they have good reason to be, but I wasn't about to take the chance that Robin wasn't going to do something stupid."

"Like what? Pull out a gun? A knife? Turn into a giant bird?"

As soon as she said it, she wished she hadn't.

Out here, with the wind blowing in off the prairie, standing in the middle of a town that shouldn't exist, it didn't sound quite so preposterous as it should have.

"Don't worry about it," he said, taking out his flashlight, holding her arm with his right hand as he guided her around the corner into the alley. "This is still Missouri territory, remember?"

It took her a moment: "Show me, right?"

He nodded. "Absolutely."

"But you won't be surprised if they do."

He didn't answer.

He didn't have to.

*   *   *

The buildings on either side of the alley cut off most of the wind. And most of the light.

The flashlight beams and their side-glow pressed much of the dark aside, but not nearly enough for Vivian's peace of mind. Their footsteps were too loud; their breathing was too loud; the walls that formed the alley were too high, too sickly grey no matter what their real color was.

When she eased to one side and his hand left her arm, she watched him touch his jacket, just once, a gentle pat. A reassurance of his weapon. She didn't need to do the same. She could feel its weight, right where it belonged, and knew she could have it out before he had a chance to blink.

She never bragged about her skills, not even to herself. That she used them rarely didn't matter; when she had to, she could. That had been enough for Taylor Blaine, and by his attitude, it was apparently enough for Proctor as well.

She wished that made her feel better.

The Old West ended and the real world returned, and with it the wind, slipping through backyards, giving voice to chimneys. Leafless branches vibrated stiffly, but not always silently. She could feel dust against her cheek, could almost feel it settling into her hair.

And something else, something damp.

She looked up and realized half the stars were gone, and many of the others had paled considerably.

Great; just great.

The clouds she had noted on the horizon earlier had finally reached Hart Junction, and while there was no thunder, no lightning, she didn't think, when the storm broke, it would be a gentle shower.

She moved more quickly, and Proctor kept up. Saying nothing. Using his flashlight to touch blank windows, ragged hedges, on both sides of the alleys they passed through. When they reached the third block, he moved closer, an arm's length, no more, and they rounded the corner and headed for the car.

"You know," he said, his voice startling her, "I almost expected to see the damn thing gone."

"Where would they take it?" she said. "Stick it in the middle of a cornfield?"

"Why not?"

"You weren't watching while you were driving, were you? Proctor, there *are* no cornfields out here. There's nothing out here but grass and this town."

Just at the edge of the streetlamps' reach, the car seemed touched with phosphorescence. The side windows glowed, and the chrome trim looked like etched silver.

If you start on your own, she told it, I don't give a damn, I'm gonna scream.

Proctor reached into his jeans pocket, and she heard the muffled jingling of the keys. A comforting sound, and she decided that as soon as they got in, she was going to turn on the radio, and turn it on loud. Only then would she bother to switch on the heater.

She almost told him that, hoping to make him smile; instead she grabbed his arm, made him stop.

The car was still a good two houses away.

He looked at her: *what?*

She pointed her flashlight at Leona's house. The beam didn't reach that far, but he got the point and he looked.

She kept her voice low, not quite a whisper: "We left the lights on."

There were any number of explanations, and probably most of them were perfectly reasonable; nevertheless, Vivian tugged Proctor's arm gently, directing them into the middle of the street. More room to maneuver; more room to run.

More room to fight.

Proctor took out the keys and slipped them into his jacket pocket, keeping his right hand free. He had slowed, but not much, his stride shorter, more cautious. With hand gestures, he told her to keep an eye on the car, while he kept an eye on the house.

Her impulse was to remind him, sharply, that she knew how to do her job; her reaction was to ignore him and stare at the front porch as they drew closer.

The problem was those stupid plaster figures on the other side of the hedge—they kept drawing her attention away from the house. They weren't perfectly visible, thanks to the feeble reach of the street-light, yet they were visible enough as blobs and sticks of shadow to interfere with her concentration. Even the flashlight didn't help. It only created shadows, and made them jump as she walked.

The wind punched her spine, shoving her forward. She cursed silently and half turned to keep her balance, and cursed again when Proctor's flashlight went out. He shook it angrily, rapped it hard against his palm, and jammed it into his hip pocket. A tap to her shoulder asked her to sweep her own light over the top of the hedge as they approached it.

His manner made her more nervous than she thought she ought to be. While it certainly didn't hurt to be wary, just because the lights were out didn't mean they were going to be ambushed. Not with guns, at any rate; they would have been used a long time ago, as soon as she and Proctor had been in range and in the sights.

They had just reached the edge of Leona's property, when her own flashlight dimmed, and nothing she did made it brighten again. Now it barely reached the hedge, and she switched it off in disgust.

And one of the figures near the porch moved.

At first she thought it was a mind trick. The wind, afterimages left by the flashlight, the tension. Look away, look back, and the illusion would fade.

It didn't.

Proctor's stance told her he had seen it, too.

A formless bulge of black near the corner of the porch, growing slowly above the figures around it. Spreading. Rising. Winking flecks within of silver, maybe gold.

One of them, she thought as she drew her gun; one of those men, back from the search.

A distant echo of a distant voice she had heard several times before: Lesson One—if you draw your weapon, make sure you're going to use it.

When she cocked the hammer, the sound startled Proctor, but he didn't protest.

The shadow rose, above the figures now, and it took a moment before she realized it was floating. Still rising. Slipping into the black where the stars once had been, and again she had to wonder if it had been her imagination.

Until, a moment later, she heard the unmistakable sound of slow-beating wings.

"What the hell?" she said, squinting at the sky.

"I don't know," he answered.

He didn't, she didn't, and she didn't want to, not right now. She slapped his shoulder lightly to urge him to the car, took one step after him, and froze when the streetlight shattered into a shower of sparks and glass.

NINETEEN

Instinctively Proctor lifted a hand to protect his eyes, even though the exploding light was half a block away. He'd heard no gunshot, just the electric pop of the bulb, but the last thing on his mind right now was how it was done.

They had to get to the car.

They had to get inside.

The keys were in his hand when he began to run, a clumsy gait because his vision was confused with the street as it had been, and the street as it now was. Darkness wasn't total, but it was deep enough to prevent him from going as fast as he wanted. At the moment he dared no more than a slow trot.

The wind didn't help either, growling and trying to shove him off-balance, while the cold seemed to turn his face into stiff paper.

Above him, above the wind, the wings, slow and heavy.

Vivian kept close, their shoulders brushing now

and then. Her breathing was unsteady, as if she'd catch it in order to speak, and change her mind.

An unseen depression in the blacktop made him stumble; she snared his arm and held him, and they spun in an erratic circle, clutching at each other until they could move again.

Another dip, and she missed him this time. He skipped sideways, one arm flailing, until he forced himself to stop before he tripped.

Standing alone in the dark, in the wind, ordering calm before he started off again, slower this time, a burgeoning cramp between his shoulders as the muscles tensed in expectation of something striking.

"Come on!" Vivian snapped, half in anger, half in fear.

Cold burned his lungs; sweat broke across his brown.

He was pretty sure he could see the outline of the car just ahead, and yelled, "Jesus!", when his left knee slammed into the front bumper and he sprawled across the hood, listening to the keys skitter across it to the street.

Above him, above the wind, the wings, slow and heavy.

On hands and knees they scrabbled frantically until his fingers closed around the chain. A relieved smile, an extended hand, and they grunted to their feet, embarrassed for each other at the fear they felt.

His eyes widened, he whirled, and yanked her

back down as something plunged out of the dark, out of the sky, sweeping across the car roof, so close he could feel the wind of its passing.

An image of something glinting—a talon, an eye. There was nothing else, no impression of what it might be. But there was a definite impression of what it was not:

It wasn't a bird.

Still crouched beside the car, Vivian punched his arm to bring him back, and said, "The next time, I'm using it," and held up the gun.

At this point he didn't care. Using the thumb and forefinger of his left hand as a frame for the lock so he could find it without fumbling, he unlocked the door and backed away clumsily to get it open without standing. The interior roof light let him see Vivian's face, and he couldn't tell whether she was terrified or angry. He suspected a little of both.

"In," he said.

Immediately, she scrambled in and over the driver's seat, nearly spilling herself into the well below the glove box as she tried to sit.

Proctor rose to follow, heard the wings at his back and swung himself against the side of the car, one hand gripping the doorframe, as the creature dove at him again, swift and silent.

Talons curved and sharp were all he managed to glimpse as they swiped at his face, caught the car roof instead and made him shudder at the scream of gouged metal. As Vivian screamed, "For Christ's sake, get in!", he uncoiled to his feet, gun in hand, and braced himself against the roof.

Fired twice into the dark, in the direction he thought it had taken.

"Proctor, damnit!"

"Headlights," he yelled back, twisting to face the trunk, and the headlights flared, the taillights glowed fire and he saw it sweeping low, not three feet above the road, swerving sharply, caught in the red glow for only a second but just long enough for him to fire again, three times more as he swiveled to trace its flight.

This time it screamed.

A long, low, deep-throated scream torn by the wind, fading as he tried to follow its direction.

"My God," Vivian said as he jumped in behind the wheel, switched on the engine and let the car roll forward.

"Window," he said, rolling his down. Listening "Where is it, damnit, where is it?"

"Proctor—"

He shut her up with an impatient slash of his right hand, his head nearly out the window. Listening. Squinting into the wind, eyes tearing. Ahead; he was pretty sure it was straight ahead, but the engine and the wind made it difficult to—

"There," Vivian said, much too calmly.

Just above the glow of the headlamps, at the end of their reach, he saw a dark shape wobbling, its long wings tilting it clumsily left, then right. A surge, and it rose; another scream much less powerful, and it sank. Swung out of the light and into it again. Pulled ahead of it and fell back.

When it touched ground, Proctor braked and opened his door.

"Where are you going?" Vivian demanded.

With gun still in hand he walked toward it, feeling nothing as the great wings folded, rippled, blurred, and a woman in monk's robes staggered forward a few paces before she fell onto her face.

The sound of her skull hitting the street made him wince.

The echo of her winged screams became the roar of the wind.

Warily, veering slightly to stay out of reach, just in case, he watched the figure for signs of movement. But there was too much blood trailing behind her, pooling at her side, matting her blond hair. By the time he reached her, he had put the gun away, put his hands in his jacket pockets and mentally apologized to Hazel for thinking her belief a sham.

Vivian joined him hesitantly, trying to watch him and the fallen woman at the same time.

"I saw it," she said, voice taut with the effort to remain calm. "Tell me I saw it."

"You did," he told her.

She shook her head quickly. "No. I couldn't have." She looked back to the car, and he knew what she was doing—trying to figure out how the woman had done it. It wasn't by flying; that was impossible. There had to be another explanation, and for her sanity, she needed to find it.

He couldn't help her.

More often than not his work unearthed the likes of Elizabeth Savage's ghost-nephew. He expected it. He counted on it. It was the way of most things.

Yet, as he'd told her, there was always Missouri in the back of his mind—show me.

And once in a very great while, like tonight, he was shown.

In a very different way, he expected it.

He counted on it.

Vivian, if she was going to spend time on his special cases, would have to learn the difference.

For her sanity.

She looked at him helplessly, begging for an explanation. He knelt by the woman, avoiding the blood, and turned her head to one side. It wasn't Robin, the mocking one; it was Lark.

Jesus, he thought; is there more than one?

He stood, wondering, listening for the wings of Lark's companions. A grunt, and he leaned over. "Help me," he said, grabbing the woman's arms. "Take her legs."

Vivian didn't move.

"Vivian, we have to get her out of sight." He nodded toward Leona's house. "Behind the hedge. Quickly."

She didn't move until he had already dragged the body a couple of steps. Then, with a shudder, she grabbed Lark's ankles, and they half dragged, half carried her around the mouth of the hedging and left her in the dark.

Back in the car, he turned the heater's fan on as high as it would go. It wouldn't be enough to stop the chills Vivian felt, but it would help. A momentary placebo, until she stopped chasing after her thoughts and let them catch up.

"It is almost always," he said as he drove to the intersection and turned left into the alley, "a punch in the gut, you know. Seeing one, even if you suspect there is one."

"You expect this?" she asked, her voice abnormally high.

"No. Never. Because it's too seldom true."

Her mouth opened. Closed. Opened again, and stayed that way until he reached the main street and stopped, the engine idling. To the east they could hear the growl of approaching engines: the hunt was over.

"What now?" She looked up the street. "Do you think they know? What we saw, do you think they know?"

He shook his head. "I don't know. Maybe, like Hazel, some of them believe it might be, but I doubt any of them really believe."

"We should tell them."

He was tempted to agree. But: "Even if we do, so what? I have a feeling we'd only get more stories. And personally, I'm a little sick of their stories."

"So . . . what?"

"So . . . I vote we go straight to the source, before Lark's people find out what's happened."

She blinked at him. "The ranch? You really still want to go to the ranch?"

No, he answered; no, I really do not.

"Yep."

"You're crazy."

He smiled that one-sided smile. "Just pretend we're the cavalry coming over the hill."

"That's stupid."

"Okay. But we're going anyway." The smile faded. "It's where the answers are, Vivian. Most of them."

She tilted her head, acceptance if not agreement. "And when we get there? If there are . . . ?" She waved a hand, uncertain.

"Shape-shifters," he said. "If there are more, we defend ourselves."

That she understood, but as he swung into the street, he could see in the corner of his vision the way she stiffened in her seat. It wasn't preparation for an upcoming fight; it was preparation for what she might be fighting.

They passed the Gold Star.

Hazel Platt stood in the doorway.

He gave her a solemn nod. Her expression didn't change, but he knew she had heard the fight—she had a shotgun in her left hand.

A curling wave of dust blew across the road as they took the low rise to the railroad tracks. Vision obscured, Proctor slowed, and for a moment the Junction was gone in the rearview mirror, nothing ahead but the pale twin beams of the headlamps.

It made the prairie twice as large, twice as imposing.

Twice as empty.

"Tell me something," Vivian said.

"Sure. What?"

"Anything." She shifted, and for the first time he noticed the gun lying across her lap. Her right hand covered it lightly. "Do you know what we're getting into?"

"Where?" he said, checking behind them again. "At the ranch, or . . ." and he jerked a thumb over his shoulder.

He had been watching as headlights flowed into the street, too flared at this distance to distinguish individual vehicles. But one of them, after stopping for a few seconds, moved on, and he supposed Hazel had told someone which way he had gone.

"Now what?" she grumbled.

"We'll find out soon enough," he answered calmly, even as he pushed the accelerator down. If they wanted to get into a chase, they were going to have to work a little before they caught him.

And he did want them to catch up.

Which they did, about a mile later.

A pickup roared up to their rear bumper and hung there, headlights filling the car, nearly blinding him. It was an invitation to pull over, and when he refused, the truck suddenly roared ahead and stopped in the middle of the road, its hood pointed to the shoulder.

Proctor braked carefully and sat there without switching off the engine or the lights.

Vivian slipped her gun out of sight.

The truck was angled away from them, and he couldn't see who was in the passenger seat. But a big man in a sheepskin coat walked around the bed, squinting in the headlights, his left hand in his pocket. The truck's engine still ran; exhaust puffed out of its pipe.

Proctor rolled the window down when the man reached him. "Evening," he said pleasantly.

The man leaned over, one hand braced on the window well. "Mr. Proctor, Mr. Wayman would appreciate your coming over to have a word with him."

Proctor, his hands still in clear view on the steering wheel, shook his head. "I don't think so. It's cold out there."

Marlin Bliss leaned closer, his left hand exaggerating movement in his pocket, a supposed indication that he was armed. His breath steamed into the car. The side of his face caught part of the dashboard's green glow. "I don't think that's the right answer, Mr. Proctor."

Proctor heard the faint click of his passenger door unlatching. "It's the only answer you're going to get. He wants to talk to me, he can come over here."

Bliss shook his head in disappointment, sighed with feigned regret, and backed off a step as he pulled out his gun, a small revolver which, from Proctor's viewpoint, had a hell of a large barrel.

"Out, Proctor, now. Move it. I don't have time for your shit."

The passenger door opened, and Vivian slid out quickly, silently, and from the light thump he heard on the roof, he guessed that she had braced her gun hand on the car.

"What the hell do you think you're doing?" Bliss demanded uncertainly.

"My job," she answered coldly.

When Proctor heard the unmistakable cock of a hammer, he thought, Jesus Christ, she's going to kill him.

TWENTY

In the rearview mirror Proctor saw silent explosions of lightning deep in the clouds just west of town, flashes of vivid color that only accentuated the night. He heard no thunder. There was only the constant wind, and the faint hiss-and-scratch of blown dust against his door. Five yards away, the truck in the car's headlights seemed false, something pasted against the flat black of the sky.

Carefully he opened his door, watching Bliss back away, his weapon still out but his expression unsure.

Zipping his coat up, Proctor squinted against the blowing dust, left the door open and walked toward the truck. As he passed the rancher he said, soft and low, "Don't try it, it isn't worth it, she'll blow your head off," and walked on without looking back.

As soon as he reached the cab, he slipped in behind the wheel, shifted until his back was against the door, and said, "Wayman, just what the hell do you think you're doing?"

Ike Wayman gaped at him, blinking rapidly, clearly unused to having the game taken to him.

Proctor held back a sigh. "Let's keep this short. I don't want to be out here any longer than I have to. Are you going to talk, or am I?"

Wayman sputtered and blustered before settling on looking indignant, until Proctor reached over and ran a finger down the sleeve of his coat.

"Nice," he said. "Expensive. Tailored suit. Silk tie. Diamond ring." He stared through the windshield for a moment. "For a one-bank banker in a town of less than thirty, you're doing all right for yourself."

"I don't—"

Proctor leaned closer; the man shifted away.

"You're buying up houses, property, whatever else there is for sale around here. And I have the distinct feeling it's not your money." A quick, mirthless smile. "Leb told his story well, Wayman, but I also get the feeling you don't care if I kill the shape-shifters or not." He faced front. "In fact, I'm not supposed to."

Wayman looked desperately over his shoulder, but could only see Bliss standing helplessly in the road.

"I'm supposed to die, aren't I, Mr. Wayman."

In the glare of the headlights, in the cold, the banker's thin lips tightened. His jaw worked. A faint glint of perspiration.

"I don't know who they are," he said weakly, offering a defense. "I swear I don't."

Proctor looked out the windshield again, shifting away from the door, one hand on the steering wheel, the other on the door's handle. He was less angry at Wayman than he was furious with himself, for allowing this to happen. Conned into a death trap by a bunch of actors who were terrified of their own shadows. That he couldn't have known ahead of time was no excuse; at least not now.

"What are these things?"

Wayman looked out his window, shook his head. "I don't know. They just . . . came. Morning Star, I mean. One day they weren't here, the next they were. We didn't know about . . . about the other until later." He looked at Proctor. "We didn't know, I swear to God. We didn't know."

"But you didn't stop working with them."

Wayman's smile was more a grimace. "You don't know their leader, Mr. Proctor. Very persuasive. Very . . ." He hesitated. "Seductive."

Proctor's hands twitched, fingers flexed.

"It isn't working out," he said, almost to himself. "There are people dying—*dying*, Mr. Wayman—who aren't supposed to." He turned his head. "Am I right?"

"Otis . . . he wouldn't sell."

"So you had him killed."

Wayman looked horrified. "What? No! Good Lord, man, no. I was going to talk to him tomorrow. Double the offer. If . . . if he didn't take it, I knew . . . I was pretty sure Merle would, if I promised her lots of light." His left hand drifted to his chest, his eyes closed briefly. "Merle."

"You should go to the house," Proctor said mildly. "Really. You should see what's left of her."

Wayman moaned.

"She was an old woman, I'm told." He shook his head. "You should see it. You should see all that blood."

"My God," Wayman yelled, "it wasn't supposed to happen this way!"

"No. It never is."

They sat in silence for several seconds. The truck shimmied in a gust; the fan blew heat over their legs.

"How many joined Morning Star?"

Wayman jumped as if Proctor had jabbed him.

"How many?" Proctor repeated.

"I don't . . . I'm not sure. Not many. A few."

"They left, you never saw them again, right?"

Wayman nodded.

"Kenny's wife? Leb told me something about what happened. Is that true?" His voice hardened. "Or is that another one of your goddamn stories."

"It's—" Wayman sighed, and appeared to shrink inside his coat. "It's true."

"And you never called the police."

He could see another defense forming, another rationalization to prevent his fee, whatever it was and whatever it was called—and whoever was paying it—from turning into blood money.

The effort failed.

Wayman waved a weak left hand, let it flutter into his lap.

Persuasion; seduction.

The money was real; nothing else mattered.

"God, you're something else," Proctor said, almost as weary as he was disgusted.

He thought then of those old movies, of the villains who had, in their own twisted way, a sense of honor; he thought of those old movies, and how the hero would leave the villain alone in a room. With a gun. How he would walk away and wait for the sound of the single, telling shot.

He looked over at Wayman and knew there was no honor here.

He turned off the engine and yanked the key from the ignition.

"Hey," Wayman said, startled, surprised.

Proctor slid out, leaned back in and said, "It's not all that far. A mile, maybe, right? About how far Kenny's wife had to go."

He slammed the door on the banker's yell and walked slowly toward the car. Bliss watched him warily, backing away as he approached, fists helpless and trembling at his sides. Watching him. Watching Vivian. Trying to decide if now was the right time.

Proctor smiled and shook his head, bounced the keys in his palm, and deliberately turned his back to open the car door, making sure he stayed out of her line of fire.

"When I get in," he said quietly, "count to three, then join me."

"Do I kill him?"

It was tempting.

"No. He's already dead."

After a moment's hesitation, Bliss raced for the truck as Proctor drove away, speeding up only slightly as he rounded the truck's rear bumper, listening to the man's enraged shouting, listening to Wayman's equally angry response.

Vivian looked back. "All they have to do is sit in there and wait for the sun to come up."

Lightning danced in the clouds.

"Yep."

She faced front. "You don't think they will?"

"It doesn't matter. Merle was attacked from the inside."

"You—" She turned again, quickly, and grabbed the back of her seat. "Proctor, you can't."

He didn't look, didn't slow down, didn't bother to say, *oh yes I can*; he concentrated on the dark road ahead, keeping the window down, trying to listen above the rush of wind the car made, the rush of wind that barreled out of the sky. It was futile; he knew it; he did it anyway.

He couldn't hear the wings, but he hadn't gone a hundred yards before he heard the first scream.

This time he did look, glancing in the rearview mirror at the spot of white light back there in the night. He couldn't see movement, but he heard another scream, and a gunshot, a second one, before he faced front again.

"Maybe," he said, "they'll be all right."

Vivian didn't answer. She stared at the weapon in her hand, then put it away as fast as she could. Took several deep, shuddering breaths.

Gunshots, and screams.

"Please, close the window."

He didn't, but he drove faster.

"For God's sake, Proctor."

"I told you a long time ago how it works."

"But this is murder!"

Gunshots.

"Yes," he said. "I suppose you could look at it that way."

The dark room.

The blue light.

A figure stood by the black pedestal and stared at the shattered bell jar on the floor.

At the shards of dull amber that lay scattered at its feet, dropped because the figure's hands had been too nervous to hold it tightly.

The figure knelt, hands trembling as they passed over the crystal's pieces. Picking a piece up, trying to fit it to another. Faster. And faster still. Until frustration brought it to its feet, enraged. It flung the pieces it held against the wall, then kicked out, scattering glass and the amber into the dark beyond the blue.

When it screamed, it was a woman's scream.

When it screamed again, it wasn't human.

"Proctor," Vivian said in startled amazement, "I think they're coming."

In the mirror he saw headlights approaching fast, and braced himself, noting as he did that she had drawn her weapon again.

Soon the cab filled with glaring white, forcing him

to squint until the vehicle pulled sharply into the left lane and sped past them without slowing, without stopping. It was an automobile, and he couldn't tell who was driving, but he had a glimpse of what he thought was a backseat packed to the windows with clothes and cartons.

Then there was nothing but trailing red lights that lasted for a long time before the night took them.

"They're not waiting," she said, twisting around to see if there was anyone else. "They're not waiting to see how it turns out."

"Would you?"

"Conscience?"

"Self-preservation. Those shifters, whatever they are, seem to be out of control."

She frowned. "How do you figure?"

He only looked pointedly at the rearview mirror, reminding her of Wayman and Bliss, the apparent local leaders of the charade.

Vivian swiped idly at her lapels. "This isn't going to be one of those things, is it? We're not going to try to capture one and bring it back to study, are we?"

His laugh was staccato and deep before he said, "Are you out of your mind?"

Ahead he could see a single light glowing off to the right. The Coglin ranch, he assumed. There was nothing else out here but black. There was also no sense trying the sneak-attack approach. Morning Star must have seen him driving away from the truck, and they weren't so inhuman as not to figure out where he was headed. They might even have guessed his plan, which wasn't complicated at all: get inside, find out as much as he could, and get out without getting himself or Vivian killed.

The single light became two, then three, then what looked to be a double line. A barbwire fence, sagging in places, lined the road and eventually led to an open, wide gate topped with an arch with a trio of painted white horseshoes nailed to the center.

At the entrance he stopped, running his palms lightly around the steering wheel.

One hundred yards beyond the arch the unpaved road widened to accommodate two vehicles. On either side, every twenty feet or so, a black-frame carriage lamp burned softly atop a rounded, white-painted post set in concrete. Past the last one, the road forked. To the left it skirted a fair-size lawn and disappeared around the side of the ranch house, presumably to a garage and the outbuildings behind; on the right it led to a crushed-stone parking area marked by a split-rail fence.

The house itself was long, white, and one-story, with a peaked roof, and a porch that ran the structure's width. Even at this distance, in this light, it appeared freshly painted, the several windows flanked by dark shutters, a yellow bulb burning over the front door in the center. All the windows were dark.

He lifted his foot off the brake, the car idled forward, and Vivian reached out to grip the dashboard lip as if they were speeding.

She opened her mouth to say something, shook her head, changed her mind.

Proctor touched the accelerator, held it down, and watched the windows, the door, the corners of the house as they bumped along the drive. The wind had eased, and he could hear nothing but the engine and the crunch of the tires over the hard-packed dirt. He rolled his shoulders. He licked his lips and swallowed dryly.

"Proctor."

"It's easy—we go in, one way or another, we look around, we get out."

"You have to know that badly?"

"Don't you?"

She didn't answer.

He reached the fork and didn't stop—the car jounced over the lawn and plowed through the grass when he spun the wheel and braked, facing the car toward the drive. Vivian was out before he stopped, sprinting for the door. She had her hand on the knob when he reached her, his own gun in hand.

She hesitated.

He nodded for her to go ahead.

She opened it, and stepped aside.

Another nod, and he went in, found a wall switch and flicked it up.

"Damn," Vivian said. "Would you look . . . damn."

TWENTY-ONE

They stood in a square, slate-floor foyer, faded
rectangles on the walls where pictures or mirrors
once hung. An overhead light was barely strong
enough to reach the living room straight ahead.

But it was enough.

To their immediate right, through a wide archway,
was a room whose walls were covered with shelves,
the glossy-top refectory table in the middle covered
with books open and closed, and two large globes,
one of which had a ragged hole punched into the
Pacific Ocean. He didn't bother to go in, because half
the shelf books were on the floor. A quick check from
the threshold told him most of them were refer-
ences—encyclopedia and atlases, paperback round-
ups of various years and college texts that seemed to
cover most of the sciences.

They were all ripped to shreds.

A second wall switch lit an oval chandelier in the
center of the living room; most of the bulbs had been
smashed. The furniture had been overturned, cush-
ions gutted, and what had been on the walls had

been flung aside and slashed or stamped on. Broken lamps and twisted shades. A heavy oak coffee table nearly split in half. The smell of scattered ash from fireplaces that faced each other across the room on the east and west walls.

Proctor mimed tossing a coin, and made his way to the right, stepping over a toppled end table missing two legs, almost tripping over a poker with a sword-hilt grip. He picked it up, hefted it, and crossed the raised brick hearth, where he found another switch, this one lighting a narrow hall that led toward the back. Torn paper, broken-spine books, more fireplace ash.

"Man," Vivian said, not bothering to lower her voice. "Somebody lost her temper."

A bedroom to either side, small, spare, only cots and dressers, none of which had been touched. They checked the drawers, which were empty, and under the cots. In each of the rooms' single closets hung two robes; no footwear, nothing on the shelves but a fine layer of dust.

There were no toiletries in the bathroom at the end of the hall, one set of embroidered guest towels, one matching washcloth.

"I don't get it," she said as they made their way back to the living room. "They don't brush their teeth or shower?"

He didn't know, couldn't begin to speculate. At least four women lived here, but it didn't look as if any living had been done.

"How much time?" she wondered, picking her way across the floor.

"I don't know. If they find Lark . . ."

A hall on the living room's north side took them into a kitchen, modern and clean, its cupboards above and below holding dishes, glasses, a few tins, a few boxes of ready-mix meals. There was only enough silverware for two. Only the refrigerator was packed, mostly vegetables and fruit. No milk, no soda, no beer or wine.

"Proctor," she said when they returned to the hall, "I don't want to think what I'm thinking."

"Look for a cellar door," was all he said.

"Blaine doesn't pay me enough to go into a cellar in a place like this."

Past the kitchen was another door, this one leading to a second bathroom, much smaller than the first, that looked as if it had never been used.

But there was an odor now, vague and vaguely familiar.

Vivian wrinkled her nose, puzzled, but shrugged when he looked at her to see if she knew what it was.

Another door was already open.

They didn't go in.

It had been a study once, or an office. Now it looked like a demolition site, its stout walnut desk heavily scored as if by a dozen knives, the shelves cleared, some yanked clear of the wall. A computer terminal had been flung against the wall with such force that it stuck in the plaster, up near the ceiling; a keyboard had been bent in half and tossed onto a pile of gutted books and manuals; the ceiling fixture had been yanked out, leaving a great gap in the ceiling, and dangling wires. Near the door were the remains of a large-button telephone.

The smell grew stronger when they reached the end of the hall. The door here was thick, with a heavy iron latch instead of a knob. It fit into its frame as though it had been carved into the wall.

Proctor touched the latch, half-expecting it to burn him, thinking, *Kira Stark's body has never been found.*

The latch handle was heavy and worn smooth, and he raised it with some difficulty.

Merle Dugan.

The door swung open smoothly. Silently. Nearly six inches thick. A single bulb over the door on the inside winked on, not quite strong enough to reach all the corners on the far wall. The floor was made of large blocks of marbled stone.

Hazel stood in the saloon window, watching the street, her shotgun braced against the sill. It hadn't been all that long, she thought, but it was taking a hell of a long time for Ike to get back. A few people had stuck around, standing by their cars, leaning against their trucks, smoking, joking nervously. Now and then checking the storm's progress.

Afraid to go home.

Afraid to stay where they were.

Lightning washed the street; the wind finally brought the smell of coming rain.

Behind her, Kenny Stark berated Leb for getting so

drunk, and Leb, at last awake, couldn't make him shut up so he could find out what was going on.

"Hazel," he pleaded, "will you call off this mutt?"

She didn't turn.

"Dot," he begged. "For God's sake, will you do something here?"

Dorothy Holland sat at the piano, picking out one-finger tunes for her son, who huddled beside her on the bench. She had barely spoken a word since she'd come in, dragging a protesting Timmy behind her. Nothing but, "I heard them," and asked if Hazel had another gun.

I'm going to hell for this, Hazel thought; dear Lord, I'm going to hell.

Suddenly a car raced out of the alley, barely avoiding striking the others as it slammed to a halt, and Zona Temple got out. Except for Marlin Bliss, he was the largest man in town, but right now Hazel thought he looked no older than Timmy. He pointed at the sky, at the alley, back to the sky, and ran to the Gold Star, punching through the swinging doors, stopping when he saw Leb sitting on the bar.

"What?" Leb demanded in full ill temper.

Temple said, "I saw them."

"What do you mean?" Hazel asked, reaching for the shotgun.

"Over by Leona's. I saw them." He pushed a hand back through his hair. "He got one of them, Haze. That Proctor guy, he got one of them. And they found her."

Dorothy played the piano.

Timmy sang softly: *Twinkle twinkle, little star.*

"Aw, shit," Leb said. "Aw, *shit!*"

The street was already empty.

"Haze," Zona said, "I'm leaving. I'm guessing most of them are. I ain't even going home. Any of you folks want to come, I'll take you. But it's got to be now, you understand? It's got to be now."

How I wonder what you are.

"Count me in," Leb said, sliding off the bar. He grabbed Kenny's shoulders and shook him. "Kenny, we're getting out, you understand me? We're getting out."

Kenny blinked at him stupidly, and Leb rolled his eyes, turned him around and pushed him gently toward the door. "Go with Zona, okay? You go with Zona."

Up above the world so high.

Hazel stepped away from the window. "Too late," she said, her voice unnaturally calm. "Too late."

"Oh, God," Proctor whispered as the stench overtook him.

He couldn't move. Swallowing against the bile that rose toward his throat, he took a lurching step, and couldn't move again.

Muttering a vicious curse, Vivian brushed past him, glared at the bulb, and examined the floor as she made her way around the room, keeping close to the wall. He followed, feeling foolish, noting that the floor dipped gently toward an open drain in its center, like a funnel.

The source of the smell.

The walls were smooth, painted midnight blue, and had no signs of distress.

"They brought them in here," she said, looking to him for confirmation. "They . . ." She pointed her gun at the drain; unlike her voice, it didn't waver. "It ran into that."

The floor wasn't marbled at all; the dark lines were dried blood.

Proctor, breathing through his mouth as much as he could, moved sideways to the rear wall, staring at the drain, staring at the dark paint, finally deciding something wasn't quite right about this. It was an educated guess, no more than that, but the room didn't seem nearly deep enough to take up the rest of the house's length.

When he spotted the seam, he grunted.

"What?" she asked.

"Door."

Once he was able to outline the door with his fingers, he pushed in its center, and it too swung open smoothly, without a sound.

A soft blue light drifted over the threshold.

Immediately, the hair on the backs of his hands stirred, and a tingling began to crawl up his arms. Electricity, he thought; faint and, as he stood there, fading.

"Go on," Vivian said. "Hurry."

He turned sharply. "What? They coming?"

"No. I just want to get out of this place. This room." In the wash of the blue light her skin was too pale, her eyes unpleasantly dark and flat. "Come on, move. We haven't got long, you said so yourself."

He moved.

Lightning; and, for the first time, thunder, as distant and solid as the Colorado mountains.

Like a diamond in the sky.

Robin stood in the middle of the street. Looking at the saloon. Smiling.

Dorothy stopped playing.

And Robin, her robes flaring, extending, cupped her hands around her mouth, and sang, "I see you, Hazel. I see you."

The blue-light room didn't take long to search. There was nothing in it but a low black pedestal, part of a broken bell jar, and pieces of what looked like amber glass.

"So what have we learned?" Proctor whispered, crouching by the pedestal, letting his fingers slip around it, nudge it, trace its rim.

The bell jar had been on here, he figured, and whatever that amber glass had once been was probably inside. He picked up a piece the size of his fingertip and rolled it around on his palm. Then he brought it close to his eyes and realized it wasn't glass at all, it was some kind of crystal.

Vivian came up behind him. "Proctor, let's go."

He rose stiffly and showed her his prize. "What do you think?"

"I think we're pushing it, okay? I think we've overstayed our welcome."

He looked around one last time, pushed vainly at the pedestal with his foot, and said, "Okay," as he grabbed a few more amber shards and stuffed them into his pocket. "Okay."

But he didn't like it.

He wanted more time, needed more time, but Vivian's insistence drew him into the drain room, where the stench made his stomach hitch. She's right, he thought as he followed her into the hall with a backward glance; this is where they took them, where they killed them, where they—

A loud banging from the front made him grab at Vivian's coat to slow her down. She refused, virtually dragging him past the office and the kitchen.

"I locked the door," she said, finally shrugging him off. "I don't like to be snuck up on."

The banging continued, a pounding that filled the house.

"We'll find the back way," he said when they reached the living room. "Go around the house."

"Nope." She stood at the end of the foyer. "You killed one, remember? We don't need silver bullets, anything like that. They're vulnerable, Proctor, not some movie creatures. So go over there, open the door when I tell you, and I'll blow the shit out of it."

Proctor stared at her in disbelief, stared at the door that jumped on its hinges at a renewed pounding, and stared at her again.

She grabbed his coat sleeve and pushed him forward. "Go on, for God's sake." She pushed him again. "And when you open it, don't forget to duck."

When he hesitated again, trying to find the words to tell her he thought something wasn't right here, something was out of place, she said, "If you don't do it, I'll do it myself, swear to God I will."

She wasn't kidding.

The pounding returned, rattling the doorknob.

Gun in his left hand, he waited for the noise to stop, then reached for the knob. At her nod, he took a breath and yanked the door open as he dropped into a crouch and braced himself for her firing.

"Damn," she said.

When he looked, the doorway was empty.

"Proctor—"

He kept the gun close to his side, opened the door all the way, and stepped onto the porch. The carriage lamps were dark; the only light slipped around him from inside.

"Proctor!"

The heavy stable doors had nearly been knocked in; this door should have been like paper to them. And they'd only use the windows as a last resort— all that jagged glass clinging to the frame . . .

The wings; it was always the wings.

Twenty feet away, Tie stood on the car roof, the wind ruffling her bangs, twisting her curls, slipping beneath her robes to give her size and shape.

She was lovely, and she was grotesque.

A glowing shadow in the wind.

"Hi," she said.

And let her wings unfurl.

TWENTY-TWO

Because of the distance and the cloudy night, it wasn't easy to see, but what little light there was was light enough.

Her robes lifted as if filled by the wind, stretched, and *blended*, into a nine-foot wingspan of what looked like midnight leather stretched between midnight bone; her skin shaded to deep grey, stiffening and cracking as if shifting into tiny scales; her face contorted to accommodate an elongated blunt chin, while a hornlike narrow ridge grew over her brow from temple to temple, sinking flat black eyes into her skull.

Her fingers became claws; her toes became talons.

Yet he could still recognize her, despite the distortions, and that was almost as bad as what she'd become.

The great wings flexed. Slowly.

No crackling of bones, no whimpers of pain.

Except for the wind, it was all done in total silence.

Proctor raised his gun as the creature rose effortlessly off the car with a slow, arrogant beat of its wings. He understood now, why she hadn't charged into the ranch house to get them when it was clear by her strength that she could have done so easily— those wings would have hampered her movements too dangerously, and he didn't believe she could move very fast on those mostly bone-and-talon legs. But he didn't understand why she hadn't attacked him as soon as he'd come out.

Like Vivian had said, they didn't need silver bullets. It was ludicrous to believe she didn't think he would shoot her.

He took a cautious step away from the door as she rose above the porch roof's overhang. Slowly. Untouched by the wind.

Watching him. Smiling.

Daring him as he took a second step to keep her in his sights, finger ready to squeeze the trigger, put an end to it now, yet momentarily torn because he had questions that wanted answering, and dead she wouldn't be able to answer.

Higher, with a single languid stroke; and even at that impossibly slow speed, he recognized the sound.

Smiling; thick lips parting to expose her teeth, sharp and long.

They grew their vegetables, he thought; they hunted their meat.

She made a noise, a grating rumbling in her throat, and he realized with a start that he hadn't been exposed for as long as he'd thought. Not minutes, only a few seconds, as though he had sidestepped into a bizarre dream where none of the usual laws applied.

Not minutes at all, but just long enough to draw him away from the door.

"Proctor!" Vivian yelled.

He whirled when he heard the second pair of wings, and saw another one sweeping toward him along the porch, in and out of the light that spilled from the windows as if caught in a series of strobic lightning flashes.

Suddenly panicked, he fired twice as he threw himself to the floor, not knowing if he had hit her, rolling against the wall and curling as it passed over him, a talon raking across his right shoulder, ripping through his jacket, opening the shoulder right across the joint.

He inhaled sharply, and stiffened against the furnace that exploded there without warning. He almost blacked out. Shook his head in an attempt to clear it and pushed awkwardly to a sitting position just as Vivian charged through the door and whirled to face the creature as it turned to get out from under the roof. The long-barrel's retorts sounded like a cannon; the answering scream sounded like a nightmare. It struck a post head-on and tumbled helplessly into the yard, *shifting* even as Tie dropped abruptly back below the roof and lashed at Vivian's face with her claws.

She ducked, but not soon enough; her cry was more surprise than pain.

Proctor stood clumsily and grabbed her arm, yanked her back, and fired, too late again.

"Are you all right?"

A stupid question, and he winced at the blood that began to slip down the center of her forehead from beneath her wind-tangled hair. When she nodded anyway, weakly, without conviction and still stunned by the blow, he transferred his gun to his left hand and sidled to the edge of the porch, keeping a post between him and the yard.

He listened.

On the grass Ariel writhed on her stomach, hips raised as she struggled to get to her hand and knees, flowing white hair lifting to join the wind, one hand trying to reach the hole between her shoulders.

She didn't make a sound; she was dead and didn't yet know it.

His right arm began to numb, his mouth suddenly dry.

He wanted to step down, get away from the house to see more of the sky to keep ambush at bay; at the same time he wanted to make a run for the car and get the hell off the ranch, out of town, out of the state.

"Proctor?"

A look over his shoulder. Vivian was slumped against the jamb, a palm pressed to her scalp, dark threads flowing over the back of her hand.

"Jesus, Proctor, it stings like hell."

"Don't move."

"Don't worry."

The wings.

Forgetting his injury, he turned back too quickly, and cried out hoarsely when his shoulder felt as if it would tear away from his neck. The shock staggered him to his knees and tipped him from the porch onto his side, a saving move as Tie swooped at his head and missed, lifted, banked, and vanished into the dark while he tried to right himself and fire.

On his back now, gun up and shaking, sweat in his eyes in spite of the cold.

Ariel had stopped moving. Except for her filmy white hair.

With his good elbow, Proctor managed to push and grunt to a sitting position. A sleeve wiped his eyes, stinging them. He blinked heavily and got to his knees. Vivian was still against the wall, her hand gripping the jamb to keep from falling, her face dark and gleaming in the porch's deep shadow.

"Up," he whispered to himself angrily. "Get up, you idiot."

Vivian laughed weakly.

He had fallen too far from the house to grab a post or the porch floor's edge for support. He grabbed at air instead, rocking back, thrusting forward until he was on his feet, unsteady but up.

It was a small victory that made him smile even as he backed toward the house. Searching the sky, watching the lightning that raced through the clouds and darted toward the ground far across the highway.

The thunder came a few seconds later, like the rumbling in Tie's throat.

He could feel rain in the air, knew it would fall

soon and Tie would escape if she didn't want to stay and fight.

He heard it then.

Not the wings.

The scratching.

Moving much too slowly—*damn it, idiot, she's on the roof*—he turned and raised the gun.

Moving much too slowly, the pain in his shoulder threatening his vision, he tried to locate her, and failed.

The wind kicked dust and hair into his eyes; he couldn't clear them because his right arm wouldn't move no matter how hard he tried—it dangled uselessly at his side, and he could feel the blood run down to his hand.

The scratching, and a rattling angry sigh.

He was too close. He had to step away so he could scan more of the porch roof, using his left arm to shield his eyes from flying grit, wondering how something so goddamn big could hide on a roof so goddamn narrow.

When he spotted her, he knew how.

She had folded her black wings about her, turning her into a shadow that moved with the wind, hiding her face from the nose down, those flat black eyes deeper shadows still.

He couldn't help it. "Who are you?"

At the same time he made sure Vivian could see him and know by where he looked where Tie was above her. When she nodded, grimaced, and nodded again, he took a breath.

"Who are you?"

The wind hit him, half turned him, and his injured shoulder brought back the fire, flaring sparks across his eyes, breaking the spell those black eyes had cast.

"Screw it," he said, and aimed.

Tie's wings snapped open impossibly fast, and she launched herself at him, screaming to drown the wind.

He fired.

Vivian fired, up through the roof.

Tie shrieked again, and Proctor dropped to his knees when she swept over him and one wing brushed his head, bringing back the sparks.

He turned to fire again, and saw her lying on the ground not five feet away. On her back, most of her shifted to human, only the wing tips flapping weakly, convulsing. Half-crawling, half-running, he scrambled to her side, studied her face, shuddered at the way her lips tried to smile. There was too much blood; he couldn't tell where she'd been hit, or how many times.

The gun fell from his hand; he couldn't hold it anymore.

"Tie," he said softly.

Black eyes blinked, and looked, and blinked slowly again.

"Titania."

She licked her lips clean of the blood that coated them. One leg drew up in pain. The wings began to fade and fold.

"Titania, who are you?"

A lopsided grin. "Morning Star."

"From where?" he asked bracing himself not very successfully against the throbbing that had taken over his right shoulder. "Tie, your leader is dead. Ariel is dead, you can tell me, it's all right."

He knew he sounded foolish, but he didn't know what else to say.

She groaned and arched her back, and a sound he thought was the sound of her dying became a rough gasping laugh.

What? he asked without speaking; what's so funny?

"Leader," she managed, while her wings folded over her and became tattered cloth.

"What about her? She's dead."

"No." She sighed, quietly and long. "Not her."

Proctor frowned. "Ariel? She's not—"

She sighed, quietly and long as her eyelids fluttered and closed, and all she said was, "Gone," before she died.

Only the wind, and the distant lightning, the distant thunder, and the childlike woman, covered in blood.

Proctor sagged back onto his heels, left hand gripping right shoulder in an attempt to seal the pain so he could think. When he heard the faint enraged screams, he thought they were echoes of all the screams he'd just heard; when they grew louder, however, he turned his head slowly, looked past the car to the road, and saw—

Wearily: "Oh, shit."

He wanted to move fast, but his body wouldn't let him; he tried to pick up the fallen gun, but his fingers refused to grip it.

It didn't matter.

Vivian came off the porch, walking. Firing deliberately. One shot at a time. Knocking Robin out of the air before she reached the lawn. One shot at a time. When the long-barrel was empty, Vivian dumped out the shells, reloaded, and kept firing as she walked toward the body. Deliberately. One shot for each step. Until she was abreast of Proctor and the gun was empty again.

When he finally looked up, he could see blood on her leather sleeve where she'd wiped it from her face. She wasn't smiling. She looked at the bodies in the yard, shook her head, and said, "It's over."

Proctor looked at Titania, and said, "I wish it was. I wish it was."

TWENTY-THREE

Vivian found a first-aid kit amid the rubble in the ranch house. It wasn't much, but it was sufficient to bind their wounds until they reached a doctor. When they were finished, reasonably cleaned up and rested enough to move without groaning, they took one last look around before getting in the car.

"I want you to know that I have a splitting headache," she said as he sped past the dark carriage lamps along the drive.

"Story of my life," he said, driving with one hand, his right arm in a makeshift sling.

She chuckled. "Not funny. Old joke."

Before they left, he had poked around the garage behind the house, found signs that a car had been parked there once, fairly recently, and wasn't there now.

Tie had said Ariel wasn't their leader, that their leader was gone. If she hadn't meant Robin, then there was a fifth one out there somewhere.

"No," Vivian said. "If it was like . . . them, she wouldn't have taken a car."

"Or him," he said.

"Whatever."

Still, he was doubtful. "I don't know. A car or a pickup would make him look like everyone else."

"They're not like everyone else, Proctor. I know. I saw them."

She tapped the face of the green-light dashboard clock with two fingers. "Look at that, will you? Man, oh man, it's not even eleven. God, Proctor, we've only been here for six hours or so."

He didn't believe it until he looked. Time, in Hart Junction, hadn't meant a whole lot. He supposed Lana and RJ would call it a record. Personally, he didn't give a damn.

They passed Bliss' pickup.

Proctor slowed down, but not much.

The truck's headlights still washed the side of the road with grey, dust sparkling as it blew across the beams. He couldn't see inside.

Vivian pointed without speaking.

On the verge was a body, or what was left of it. From the Western hat beside it, he knew it was Bliss. Farther along, he looked back and saw that the passenger door was slightly open, its window glass webbed. He wondered if Wayman's last words were, *damn it, I didn't know.*

"All right," Vivian said, slumped in her seat, an ice pack pressed to the top of her head, "so how do you figure it? Some kind of ritual? Some kind of magic thing? Or did they slip something into the food, some kind of hallucinogenic drug that flipped us out."

His head ached from the effort to keep from thinking about his shoulder. "This is just a guess."

"You don't guess, Proctor, remember?"

He smiled; it felt good.

"I'm *guessing*," he said, "that Morning Star, or whoever's behind it, provided the money for Wayman to buy up the town piece by piece. He probably got a nice share of the action for his efforts, and probably split it with those who stayed behind. I mean, why else, other than pure greed, would someone like that young woman and her son stay here? No school, no one to play with—I don't know her story, but I'd bet she needed the money.

"Desperation and greed, Ms. Chambers; always a hell of a combination.

"I'm *guessing* from what Wayman and Leb told me that Morning Star had no intention of leaving anyone alive once the deals were all complete. They were all going to die at the end, just like those who wouldn't sell, or caused some kind of trouble.

"And I'm *guessing* that when we reach town, we're not going to find anyone there anymore."

"Those aren't guesses," she told him.

"Yeah." He drove on. "Maybe."

When they reached the tracks, he stopped. There were no lights at all in the darkness that hid the houses, and only a few remained lit along the street that they faced.

"Someone," he said quietly, "brought me here, and I want to know who it is. The director."

"You don't like being conned."

He nodded. Just once.

She set the ice pack aside, dried her hand on a towel she'd laid between them. "No one does."

"This is different. Someone, this director, knew about Elizabeth Savage, that previous case." He looked at her. "No one knows about Elizabeth Savage, Viv, except her nephew and my staff. So how did Hazel know to put it in the letter? Who told her? Who knows that much about me that they could get me out here to die? For that matter," he added, "why do they want me dead or out of the way?"

"I . . . I don't know."

"Neither do I," he said, voice deepening. "Neither do I."

He took his foot off the brake.

They drove slowly through town, not much faster than a brisk walk.

The feed-store door was open, but nothing moved inside.

The Diamond Sal was dark.

He slowed even more when they reached the Gold Star. One of the batwing doors had been torn off its hinges and lay on the sidewalk; the window had been shattered outward, and there was no light inside.

He was ready to stop, but Vivian put a hand on his arm. Shook her head.

She was right, he decided. He wanted to know, and he didn't want to know. People had fled, he knew that from the packed car that had passed them before the battle, so maybe it was better that he believe Hazel and the others had escaped the Morning Star wrath.

But as he sped up, he looked one more time, and saw something just inside the entrance.

Damn, he thought.

It might have been the glint of a piece of polished metal attached to the toe of a scruffy old boot.

He wasn't sure, but he didn't stop, and he didn't go in.

A youth, once grown, should never meet the objects of his youthful lust dreams.

Let her remain a dream; it was better that way.

"Vivian," she said when the town was behind them and there was nothing out there but the night.

He frowned. "What?"

"I call you Proctor, you call me Vivian. I hate Viv. It sounds like an abbreviation for vivisection."

He grunted a laugh. "You're awfully weird for a bodyguard, you know that, Chambers?"

"The company I keep, Proctor. It's the company I keep."

The rancher who owned the property the airstrip was on asked no questions when Vivian told him to get them a doctor, that they couldn't wait for the next day. Once they were treated, by a doctor who also asked no questions, they left, and somewhere above Kansas, Proctor sat by the window and looked out at the darkness, thinking that maybe that light down there was a light in Hart Junction.

It was only on a couple of maps, and in a few old movies, a few old television shows.

A ghost town now, that would hold all the ghosts it could when that last bulb finally burned itself out.

As they were being treated, Vivian had remarked on how well he had taken all that they had been through. She claimed she probably wouldn't sleep for a month. No; for a year. In her voice was a touch of admiration, and a touch more of fear.

He hadn't corrected her, even though she was wrong.

There was something going on out there, something he didn't yet understand. The Morning Star creatures were both an isolated case of things that go bump, things he'd been investigating for years . . . and they were a link to something else. Something bigger.

That made him angry.

Not simply because he appeared to be a target of whatever that "bigger" was, but also because it meant his special cases would never be the same again. They'd be clouded, infected, by his constant wondering if they were connected to whatever that "bigger" was.

Vivian stirred in the seat beside him, uncomfortable but still sleeping, a baseball cap hiding the gauze patch that had been taped over the area where the doctor had had to shave away some of her hair to work on the wound. She had complained so bitterly he'd laughed and had been chased from the room.

He wondered now if Blaine, once he'd heard her report, would continue to insist she be his bodyguard. He hoped so, if only because without her there he would have died at the ranch. He had no doubts about it; Morning Star would have won.

She stirred again, opened her eyes sleepily and made a face when she saw him watching. "Don't you ever sleep?"

"I will. In a while."

Her eyes closed. "I hope we get home soon."

"We will."

"No. Close your eyes. Listen."

He did, and after a few seconds knew exactly what she meant.

It was the muffled thrum of the engines, their rhythmic rise and fall so subtle most never heard it. And now that he did hear it, he knew he wouldn't be able to get it out of his mind.

It was the hush of dark wings.

And there were far too many hours left to the night.

Next, in *Black Oak*

In the middle of a mild snowstorm, the telephone rings just before dawn.

"Proctor, I have news."

Instead of slamming the phone down, Proctor struggles to wake up, because he recognizes the voice. "Good news, I hope, Mr. Blaine."

"I'm not sure. But there's a man here who says he has a picture of my daughter."

In the dark, Proctor shrugs. "And . . . ?"

"It's only three years old, Proctor; the picture is only three years old." Before Proctor can respond, Blaine says, "Come now, Proctor, come right away."

He looks at the snow sticking to the window. Hell, he thinks, anyplace would be better than this. "Sure. Where are you?"

"England. I'm in England."

A call from the nursing home:

"Mr. Proctor?"

Proctor feels acid churn in his stomach. "Yes, Dr. Browning, what is it? Is she all right?"

"I can't really say, Mr. Proctor. But I think you should know that she spoke last night."

The acid vanishes; Proctor can barely breathe.

"What . . . what did she say? Is she talking now? Should I . . . I'll be right over."

Dr. Browning laughs. "No, Mr. Proctor, you don't have to come now. Unfortunately she's already returned to her . . . normal state. But the night nurse says that shortly after midnight, she was checking on your mother, and your mother sat up and said, 'Tiger's eye.' That's all. Do you know what that means?"

A memory clamors for attention at the back of his mind, but he can't bring it out. "I don't know," he answers. "Maybe, but I don't know."

"Well, I wouldn't worry about it. She was probably just dreaming."

Maybe so, Proctor thinks, but they were the first words his mother has spoken in almost ten years.

Doc Falcon sits at the dining-room table, a half dozen small pieces of amber crystal lying on a sheet of paper in front of him.

"As best I can figure," he says to Proctor, "these are part of a globe of some kind."

"Like a map?" asks Taz, poking at them with a finger.

Falcon slaps the hand away. "No, like a globe, Paul."

"Meaning what?" Proctor asks.

"Meaning I do not know what it means. But didn't

Blaine tell you that there was a crystal ball in that photograph of his daughter?"

Proctor nods.

"Good. Ask him if it's amber."

"Meaning what?"

Falcon shrugs. "Meaning . . ." He sits back, shakes his head. "Meaning, perhaps, you'd better watch your back."

SHADOWRUN

Secrets of Power Trilogy